Brian Everest

Scan the School:
Camp Fable

Book 2 in series

A series that has been in the work since 6th grade.
Thank you, family, friends, doctors, and especially my
wife, Tillie.

Oh, and you the reader. I hope you enjoy reading this book
as much as I did writing it.

Chapter 1

Danny opened the SUV door, and the smell of pine needles hit him. The crunch of leaves could be heard as his weight shifted to the ground below his feet. Immediately, he regretted that he agreed to attend summer camp. All around him were kids a head shorter than him, screaming at the top of their lungs. Summer camp appeared to be chaotic.

In every direction, there were screaming kids, woods, and log cabins. *How did I let Mom talk me into this?* He thought. First, the failed rite of passage with Pappy, and now this. *Can things get any worse?*

Just then Danny's mom nudged him with an excited smile. "There they are!" Danny's mom waved her arms high over her head. "Joyce! Joyce! Over here."

Gosh, why doesn't she go to summer camp if she's so excited? Danny thought as he glared at his mother.

Joyce saw them. "Oswald, over here," she said, grabbing a boy's hand.

Danny's heart sank as Joyce and Oswald walked toward him and his mom.

Turning to his mom, he whispered, "You didn't mention Mrs. Ryther's son is Oddball Ozzie."

Danny's mom ribbed Danny gently. "Don't you dare call him that," she whispered back through gritted teeth.

Danny and his mom straightened up as Mrs.Ryther and Oswald came closer.

Danny's mom went in for a hug. "Great to see you, Joyce!"

"Good to see you too Linda," Joyce embraced the hug before turning to Danny. "And you must be Danny! I've heard so much about you from your mom."

"Nice to meet you, Mrs. Ryther," Danny said, putting on a fake smile.

"It certainly is. Nice to meet you too. I think you know my son, Oswald."

"It's Ozzie, Mom."

"Sorry, Ozzie."

"Oh yeah, we had homeroom together last year."

Yes, Danny knew who Ozzie was. Oddball Ozzie as everyone called him. The kid was weird. He kept to himself, never looked anyone in the eyes, and the answers he gave in class were so long and drawn out. He was truly a teacher's pet.

"Oh, so you know me. "Ozzie said, weakly. "Oddball Ozzie."

"What?" Danny did his best to pretend this was news.

"Where'd you get that from?... I for one have never heard it."

"Don't play dumb Danny. I'm not dumb." Ozzie said.

"Ozzie, be nice to Danny." Mrs. Ryther scolded.

"What, like he never said it? He was in my classroom last year. For all I know he started the nickname," Ozzie declared.

"Hey man, I've never even heard that nickname before." That was a lie. Danny had heard the nickname. He even called Ozzie, Oddball Ozzie, once or twice. Danny justified calling Ozzie, Oddball Ozzie by saying everyone else was doing it.

Ozzie shrugged his shoulders at this. "Whatever…" Turning his attention to his mom, Ozzie asked. "Do I really have to do this?"

Mrs. Ryther bent down to whisper in Ozzie's ear. "We talked about this in the car. Your father and I agreed this would be good for you. You need to get out and socialize with kids your age."

Ozzie, not whispering, responded. "I socialize with kids my age."

"Without a headset on!" Mrs. Ryther scoffed.

"Look around Mom, there are no high schoolers here. Danny and I are the only two from our school."

Let's hope so, Danny thought, *I can't be seen with Ozzie at summer camp. What high school attends summer camp?*

"Oswald Stewart!" His mother bellowed.

Ozzie gulped. She used his middle name. There was no

way he was going to win the argument. Ozzie turned away from his mom and crossed his arms.

Danny had the same sentiment as Ozzie; it was stupid for him to be here. He had so many more important things to do, like find Pappy or at least see him with the locket. The last conversation Danny and Pappy had at the airport played through Danny's mind.

"Pappy, do I have to go?" Danny pleaded with Pappy one last time that day. He did his best to hold back tears. Danny felt the two of them were the closest they had been in a long time.

"I'm sorry Danny, but this part of the trip is too dangerous for you... Listen, I called your mom earlier. She said she would meet you when you land in Washington."

"...But this is my rite of passage."

"Sorry Danny Boy, I'm not budging on this one. Maybe someday you can accompany me on an adventure like this, but not today. What you've learned over the past few days about fantasy and reality being closer than what we're taught... Well, you've only scratched the surface."

Danny gave a huff. He understood though, he just began believing Pappy's stories were real. "What should I tell Mom when I land?"

"...Tell her the truth. Tell her a friend of mine needed help. She'll understand."

Danny wiped the tears from his eyes. "Okay." He did not expect to get this emotional. He felt as though he was getting to know the real Pappy. That he finally understood him. The stories he told were not lies, but rather a door to a new and strange world that Danny wanted to know more about. The two of them had started to mend their relationship.

"And Danny, take this." Pappy held up the locket. "I want you to have it... Keep your mom safe until I get back."

Danny now clutched Pappy's enchanted locket hanging around his neck. He pictured Pappy as hard as he could, but to no avail, he could not see him. *Was he okay?... Did he find Hank and get the keys? Maybe he is with Adam in Philadelphia. Is he even alive?* Danny pushed to get the last thought out of his mind. No, he was alive. Pappy had traveled the globe and been gone longer than this. *Why can't I see him then?*

Pappy had made it so easy to get the locket to work, but when Danny touched the locket…Nothing. Nothing as far as Pappy was concerned. When he touched the locket and thought of his mom, he could see her easily. Was that because they were so close in proximity or were there other reasons? Danny did not want to think about it, fearing it may take him down a dark rabbit hole that he did not want to entertain. He had to believe Pappy would be back. He had to come back. He promised.

"Danny… Danny… Earth to Danny." Danny's mom was trying to get his attention. "I said, let's go check in."

"Mom, do I really have to go?" Danny asked, pleading with his mom one last time.

"Danny, we talked about this. Pappy's not here to watch you, I have to go to China for work, and Ms. Stitz is still recovering from her hip replacement."

Danny smiled at this. *Ms. Stitz, our neighbor. It's more like I watch her these days.*

"I'm going into high school. I don't need a babysitter." Danny whined.

"Danny there's no one to even check in on you." His mother fired back.

"Ugh!" Danny exclaimed. "What if Pappy comes home? Someone should be there for him."

"Danny, it's not like he hasn't been gone before. Besides, I thought you could not stand spending time with your grandpa."

"That was before our trip!"

"What happened on your trip?"

"We bonded," Danny replied, not wanting to give anything away.

"That's always your answer when I ask." The two of them moved toward the check-in station.

"Welcome to Camp Fable, where every story has a moral!" A college-aged guy said from behind the check-in station. "My name's Chase and I am one of your totally tubular counselors,"

Oh great! Another Tobey, Danny thought. *At least I'm not stuck in a car with him.*

When Danny and Pappy started their trip last month Tobey was their uber driver on the way to Union Station.

He rambled on and on like a surfer dude. *Hopefully, this guy will not be as annoying.*

"Could I get a name?" Chase asked. Not only did he talk like a surfer but looked like one with his wavy blond hair and aviator sunglasses.

"Daniel Bennett. That's Bennett with two T's," Danny's mom said firmly.

"Where are you all from?" Chase asked.

"Meadowbrook!" Danny's mom explained. Then blurted out, "They'll be in high school this year!"

Danny snarled in frustration. *Does she have to embarrass me like this? Why does she have to tell him I'll be in high school?*

"Gnarly!" Chase shouted at the top of his lungs. "Do you wanna bunk with the other two high schoolers?"

"Excuse me?" Danny questioned.

"Yeah, you and Oz Man are not the only high schoolers here."

Danny knew there was Ozzie, but there were other kids his age. *Dang, it! Just my luck.*

"How many kids are there from our school?" Danny asked shakily.

"You two. Then another guy, and a girl." Chase smiled.

A girl? Danny gulped.

Two other people from his high school were here and one was a girl. This was Danny's worst nightmare. He was not counting on being seen with Ozzie by someone from his school. Seeing a girl from his high school when he looked like this. That was even worse.

"Uh…" Danny stood there frozen.

"Oh, they'd love to bunk with the other boy. Joyce, what do you think?" Danny's mom butted in before anyone else could respond.

"That'd be great!" Mrs. Ryther turned to Ozzie. "Doesn't that sound lovely?

With his arms crossed, Ozzie unenthusiastically said, "That sounds swell."

"Oh, you boys will have so much fun!" Mrs. Ryther said with a big smile.

Chapter 2

Danny and Ozzie trudged through the woods along the dirt path following Chase to their cabin. Neither wanted to be here at camp and Danny was dreading the fact other kids from their school were here. How many, he didn't know, but he was not prepared for this.

I can't be seen with Ozzie. If I do there goes my reputation and school hasn't even started.

"Hey bro!" Chase nodded at a counselor coming towards them.

The guy grunted at Chase as he passed them.

What's his problem? Danny wondered.

As though Chase had read Danny's mind, Chase answered what Danny was thinking. "That was my brother. If you ask me, I've got the looks in the family." Chase waited for Danny and Ozzie to laugh at this, but nothing.

Chase stopped walking. "It's a joke… Because he's, my twin."

Danny smiled to appease Chase. Chase noticed this,

smiled, and continued to the cabin.

"This stinks," Ozzie grumbled,

"Yeah, you're telling me," Danny whispered.

"We're here!" Chase exclaimed. "Cabin 6!" Chase turned the doorknob, pushing the door open. The door moved a few inches in before the bottom of the door got caught along the cabin floor. Looking down Chase gave the door another push. The door moved again, still scraping the floor.

Turning to Ozzie and Danny, Chase said, "Just have to put your shoulder into it." With that Chase drove his shoulder into the door. The door flew inward, and Chase tumbled into the center of the cabin. "See nothing to it."

Danny peered into the cabin. The inside was a little more impressive than the outside. Yes, the floor was a little warped, there were some spaces between the wall boards, and the door did not fit into the doorframe, but overall, the inside was spacious.

The log cabin had four bunk beds, one in each corner. The cabin itself was an A-frame. Danny marveled at the height of the cabin. Though what made the cabin even more awe-inspiring was the back wall. It was an entire glass wall that allowed sunlight to cover every corner of the cabin at this moment.

For a second Danny forgot about not wanting to be at camp. "Wow! This is so cool."

"It's so bright!" Ozzie did his best to shield his eyes.

Stepping into the cabin further, Danny set his backpack

on the floor next to the bunk bed closest to the glass wall. In the center of the glass wall was a sliding door. He opened the door and stepped out onto a massive deck, Ozzie and Chase followed.

Strolling to the edge of the deck Danny looked out at a crystal-clear beach below. "This is awesome."

"This is torcher," Ozzie stated, sliding in beside Danny and leaning on the railing. "No Wi-Fi, no games, not even a TV. Why did I let my parents talk me into this?"

Danny flung an arm over Ozzie's back without even thinking. "Oh, come on Ozzie, it may not be as bad as we think. Just look at that beach and that water."

Ozzie shook Danny off. "Get away man, I like my space."

"Sorry, man. I didn't mean anything by that. I just got excited looking at the view. This may actually be fun."

"Speak for yourself. I don't do water or sand."

"Okay, got it."

"Besides, Chase said, there are other high schoolers here. Why don't you go find them?"

Shoot! Danny had forgotten there were other high schoolers here. One, being a girl. *I hope no one saw us together just now.*

"Okay, boys." Chase waved, as he thundered down the steps of the deck. "I'll leave you two to unpack. When you're ready, breakfast is being served in the mess hall."

Danny gave a fake smile as he waved bye to Chase. As he waved bye, he continued to scan the beach to see if anyone was around. From what he could tell, he could not see anyone who looked to be in high school on the beach.

This was good news, now all he had to do was back away from Ozzie. No one will be the wiser that they know each other. Danny kept his eyes on the beach as he backed towards the sliding door. He stepped into the cabin.

"Ouch!"

Danny spun around.

"Sorry!" Danny apologized.

"Ow, that one hurt."

"Are you okay?" Danny asked, before realizing the person's toe he had stepped on belonged to a girl. Once he realized the person was a girl, he lost all nerve to speak.

The girl could see Danny was blushing. She smirked at this. "I'm good. Are you okay Poindexter?"

Danny snapped out of it. "Yeah, yeah… I'm fine." He said shakily.

"Okay, good. So have you seen Guy anywhere?"

"Who?" Danny had no idea who she was talking about. Was she looking for Chase?

"You know, Guy. Your bunkmate?"

"You mean Ozzie?" Danny asked even more confused.

There was a plop across the room from someone throwing their duffle bag down onto a bed. "I'm right here Dez. Sorry, I'm late."

Dez turned around. "There you are. What took you so long, Guy?"

"Sorry, I had car trouble. Better question, why are you

in the boys' cabin?"

"Looking for you. I've been here a few hours and scoped out the girls' side of the lake. Now I figure we can walk around the boys' side."

"Find anything of interest?" Guy asked, taking off some gloves.

"Not really. Nothing out of the ordinary, yet."

Danny looked towards Guy who was opening his duffle bag. It was black and in rough shape just like Pappy's enchanted duffle bag. Pappy's enchanted duffle bag in reality was a bottomless goblin bag. It could not be a goblin bag though. Pappy had told Danny humans alone could not lift a goblin bag, at least not without help.

Does he have pixie dust? Danny wondered. Then he saw them, next to Guy's bag were a pair of lifting gloves that he had just taken off.

Trying to be funny, Danny shouted across the room, "Where'd you get that bag from a goblin mine?" Danny chuckled at this.

Nothing though from Dez or Guy.

"Who's this?" Asked Guy.

Dez crossed her arms, "I don't know. He and the other one on the deck were already here when I came in."

"Yeah?" Guy took a step forward menacingly. "Well, how does he know about goblin bags?"

"I don't know," Dez said with a smile. "Think they could be one of them?"

Danny put his hands up to shield himself. "It was just a

joke.”

Dez looked around Danny to Ozzie, who was still hunched over the deck railing with his back to them. “You know that one looks a little pale. Maybe they are Water Orcs.”

Danny took a step back now frightened as Dez and Guy walked towards him. “I’m… I’m not... Not a Water Orc.” Danny stammered.

At this statement, Guy stopped walking towards Danny, but Dez kept coming.

“Hold up.”

“What now?” Dez asked, spinning towards Guy.

Danny saw this as an opportunity to run. “Ozzie run!” Danny bolted onto the deck and down the stairs. He tripped on the last two steps and fell face-first, eating a mouthful of sand.

Rolling over Danny was met with Ozzie running towards him. “You okay Danny?”

Danny did his best to get up. “I’m fine Ozzie. We have to warn the others though.”

Dez came screeching down the stairs. “See, I knew it.” She now stood in front of Danny. “They’re Water Orcs!”

Guy came running down the deck steps. Looking at Danny and Ozzie closer, he said. “I don’t think they’re Water Orcs!”

“Guy! What are you talking about, they’re Water Orcs.”

“No, they're not Dez!” Guy argued back. “Look at the necklace he’s wearing.”

Danny looked down to where Guy was pointing. The locket Pappy had given him was hanging out over his t-shirt. Quickly he tried to tuck it under his shirt collar and hide it from them.

Dez ignored the necklace, "So, what about it? So he's wearing a necklace."

"Yeah, but whose does it look like?"

Danny threw his hand over his chest. There was no way these two crazies were going to get this necklace from him. It was one of his last hopes to reconnect with Pappy.

Dez looked at Danny and then back at Guy. "I don't recognize it."

"Come on, think… Who else wears a locket like that and knows goblin bags look a lot like duffle bags?"

From Dez's facial expressions you could tell she was thinking hard. "Mr. Dailey?"

Danny's eyes grew wide. "You know my grandpa?"

"Nice try!" Dez kept coming forward.

"Dez stop!" Guy yelled at the top of the stairs.

Not taking her eye off Danny, she yelled back. "Why should I? This thing has Mr. Dailey's locket and for all we know, they have him."

"Dez!" Guy's tone shifted and Dez stopped inching towards Danny. "It's Danny! You know Mr. Dailey's grandson?"

Danny and Dez, both froze at this news.

How does he know who I am?

"How can, we be sure?" Dez asked.

"The locket. His picture is inside." Guy ran down the stairs. "Did your grandpa send you to help us?"

What is he talking about? How does he know Pappy?

Finally, Danny found the words to speak. "How do you know my grandpa? Better question, how do you know who I am?"

Chapter 3

Danny, Ozzie, Dez, and Guy sat at a table in the mess hall which was full of campers like themselves who had just been dropped off and were hungry. With all the rowdy campers surrounding them, no one would be able to eavesdrop on their conversation. The mess hall was the perfect place to discuss business, as Guy had so eloquently put it.

"Mr. Dailey didn't send you to help with the Water Orcs?" Dez asked accusingly.

"That's exactly what I have been trying to tell you. I just learned of Water Orcs this summer."

"Okay, so you have experience with them?" Guy questioned.

"Well, no… I've only heard of them mentioned in passing."

Dez let out a low *ugh* at this news. She rolled her eyes and turned to Guy. "I thought Mr. Dailey said Danny would be ready. Isn't that what his *rite of passage* was supposed to be for?" Dez put air quotes around the phrase rite of passage.

"Dez ease off, Danny… And Mr. Dailey for that matter."

Danny and Ozzie had sat there watching Guy and Dez bicker like they were brother and sister. Surprisingly though, they were not related. The two of them worked for Scan the School, the school newspaper Pappy was the advisor for. Guy was the editor and chief, and Dez was a reporter. So far, that is all Danny had been able to discern from the two of them.

As for Ozzie, he sat there shoveling food into his mouth, not saying a word. Now and then he would stop in mid-bite, put his fork down, and listen to the conversation. Luckily for Ozzie, Guy and Dez had only been focused on Danny. Drilling him with the same questions over and over.

Dez let out a big huff. "I'd ease off if Poindexter actually had any useful information on what was going on?"

"That's what I'd like to know." Danny fired back, "What is going on here? I'm here because my mom made me come. You think I want to be at summer camp?"

"Dez, Danny, will you both cool your jets!" Guy commanded. "We're not here to fight each other."

Dez crossed her arms, putting her back to Danny.

Gosh! She is insufferable! Danny thought. *The two of them may be my best lead in finding Pappy. The locket certainly isn't helping. As Mom would say, "Play nice."*

"Okay, so can the two of you fill me in on exactly why you're here? If you know my grandpa, then I'm sure you're not just here for campfires and to swim in the lake."

Dez faced Danny, "Right there, right there! It's obvious, you do not know anything. Don't go anywhere near that lake!"

"Why not?" Danny asked. Before the question had even left his lips, he knew it was a stupid question.

"Water Orcs." Danny, Dez, and Guy said in unison.

"What's a Water Orc?" Ozzie asked, before shoveling another bite of food into his mouth.

The three of them all looked in Ozzie's direction surprised. They had forgotten he was there; this was the first thing he had said since they had sat down.

"Why is he here?" Dez asked. "Should we even be discussing this in front of him?"

"Dez, it's cool," Guy reassured her. "You really want to know, Ozzie?"

"Sure."

"Promise not to freak out?" Guy asked.

"Scouts honor!" Ozzie held up the scout's honor symbol, three fingers, to signify he promised,

"You've heard of orcs, right?" Dez asked in a hushed voice.

"Yeah, those mythical creatures set in medieval movies."

"Yeah, something like that. Water Orcs are a class of orcs and... Well, they're real." Guy said.

Ozzie had his fork halfway to his mouth when he stopped moving. He froze.

Guy thought Ozzie was going to keel over at this news. To his surprise, though, he burst out laughing like a hyena.

The laughter filled the entire mess hall. The campers nearby stopped what they were doing to look where the laughter was coming from. Once Ozzie noticed people were looking at him he instantly stopped laughing, and his cheeks turned red from embarrassment.

When nothing more was said the campers went back to their own business. The chatter in the mess hall picked up again; people had forgotten about Ozzie.

"Sorry guys," Ozzie said, expecting one of the others to laugh, but all three were expressionless.

"We're serious," Dez said.

"Yeah," Danny chimed. "I didn't believe it at first, but reality and fantasy are closer than you think."

"Okay guys, good one. Let's say I play along. What is a Water Orc? What can it do? Better question: why are they here?"

"Not sure yet, though Dez and I are working on it," Guy said.

Ozzie snickered. "What do you mean Water Orcs don't just attend summer camp for swimming and campfires too."

Danny got up from his seat. "That's it, if they are really here, I'm out."

"What?!" Dez yelled. "You're turning tail and running?"

"Yeah, I'm not ready for this," Danny said, thinking back to Pappy's friend Buzz. Besides, Dez said herself, he had no useful information for them.

Plus at the first sign of trouble on his right of passage Pappy sent Danny home. Now he was at a camp with Water Orcs lurking around. His mom did not leave for China until tomorrow. He had to find a counselor and use their cell phone to call home, if he faked being sick he was sure his mom would come and get him.

"Ha! You're going to try to leave because of some made-up fairytale? One that isn't even real? Wow, you all sound crazy." Ozzie laughed.

Danny had forgotten about walking away and started to argue with Ozzie. "Ozzie you don't know what you're talking about!"

"Yes, they are real and by all means do not go near the water." Guy stated.

"Don't worry, you won't see me near the water," Ozzie assured him. "It'll either be the mess hall or our cabin."

Danny sat down. He was still thinking about leaving, but his curiosity was getting the best of him. He wanted to learn more about the Water Orcs, if anything he could leave after the conversation.

Guy continued, "Water Orcs live in the water and typically travel in pairs."

Jumping in, Dez said, "The best way to describe them is an orc, but with scales… Definitely, slimier than the ones that live on land."

"Danny, anything to add?" Ozzie asked nonchalantly.

"Nope, other than they are real. Laugh when you can." Danny replied.

"Oh, they also can multiply and shapeshift into humans, so they may start as a pair, but within a few hours they can surround you easily," Dez stated.

While Ozzie was laughing all this up, Danny was hanging on Dez and Guy's every word. With each word he thought of what he had experienced at camp already. When Dez said the Water Orcs could multiply and shapeshift he wondered if he had bumped into one of them already without even knowing it.

"Wait! They shapeshift?" The hairs on the back of Danny's neck stood up and he thought he may want to head out now after all but could not pull himself out of his seat. He had to know more. The more he knew, the closer he'd get to Pappy.

Dez rolled her eyes, "Honestly Poindexter, could you be any greener?"

Danny flung his arms onto the table, "What does that mean? Green?"

Dez laughed, "Ha, you are something!"

"Dez, lighten up. You were green once too." Guy said. "Green means new, Danny."

"Yeah, but not that green. I was more of an olive. This kid is like a stoplight green, all around *and* he's Mr. Dailey's grandson. Pathetic."

"Hey!" Danny yelled. "That's uncalled for, don't you

bring my grandpa into this!"

"Sorry, Dez said quickly. "You're right. It's just your grandpa made it seem like you knew more than you actually do. I guess though, it is not fair to compare you to him. He's a legend and a step above all of us."

Danny glared at Dez. He was too prideful to have her insult him like that. Now he was staying, now he was going to help save Camp Fable.

Turning to Guy he asked, "How do you tell if someone's a Water Orc?"

Guy thought for a second, before responding. "Well, first they're cold to the touch and their skin will be pale if they had just taken over a host."

"Yeah." Dez butted in. "That's why I thought Ozzie might be one; your pale skin." She laughed.

Ozzie's face went sour at this, he glared at Dez. "Not funny."

Dez brushed Ozzie's comment off. "The most important detail is if you see the same person twice. Two Water Orcs may shapeshift into the same person at first."

Danny gulped at this as he thought about Chase. Didn't Chase say he had a twin?

Before he could tell Guy and Dez about Chase, Danny was interrupted.

A whistle blew. "Hello, campers!" It was Chase.

"Everyone to the kickball field! Time for roll call!"

Guy, Dez, and Ozzie got up at Chase's request.

"Guys wait!" Danny yelled.

It was too late though, there was too much noise. Guy, Ozzie, and Dez exited the mess hall with the rest of the campers. Should Danny follow knowing what he knew? Were they all walking into a trap?

I've got to warm them! Danny got up from the table and slowly made his way to the front of the mess hall. *Wait! What would Pappy do? I Better not follow them.*

Danny came to a halt. He swiveled his head left and right looking for a side exit. There were bathrooms to his right; no doors there. He looked behind him. There were exits behind him but looked as though the exits were blocked by other counselors. Danny didn't know who he could trust.

Looking to his left he saw the swinging kitchen doors. Dare he exit out of the kitchen? It was his only hope. Danny raced to the kitchen, and the swinging door flapped back and forth as he ran through it. Sure enough, next to what appeared to be a walk-in cooler were a few doors.

Glancing through the windows Danny could not see any counselors guarding the doors. He figured this would be his chance to run for it. What he was running from he was not sure, but he had to keep away from Chase and the other counselors, that was for certain.

Danny crept up to a door and looked behind him as he opened the door. Before he turned around, he started running. *Smack!*

He ran right into a lanky middle-aged man which caused him to fly backward. The man bounded towards Danny.

This is it, Danny thought. He held up his arms to shield himself from what was coming next.

25

Chapter 4

"Here let me help you up." The lanky man grabbed Danny's arm and pulled him up. "Sorry about that."

Danny looked at the man. His skin was not pale nor was it cold when he touched Danny's arm.

"So-so-sorry sir." Stammered Danny.

"What are you doing over here?"

"No- No- Nothing," Danny answered, still scared.

"Well, you better get to the kickball field, Mr. Dodd is about to announce the start of camp."

Danny looked at the kickball field. That field was the last place he wanted to be. Who was he to question an adult? He tried though.

"I was, I was just going to get something from my cabin."

"That can wait. Your cabin will still be there."

Danny looked at the man, back at the field, and then at the man again.

"Go on get!" The lanky man shooed Danny along, "You

can stop by your cabin after."

Danny saw no use arguing. He figured he'd slowly walk towards the field. Once he was out of the man's eyesight then he would make a run for his cabin. Then Danny saw them, his friends. He sprinted in their direction.

"Guys, guys," he whispered. "We've gotta get out of here… Some of the counselors may be Water Orcs already."

"Keep your voice down Danny." You don't think Dez and I already know." Guy whispered.

"But guys!" Danny shrieked, as quietly as he could.

"Pipe down Poindexter and follow our lead." Dez glared at Danny, walking past him.

Danny rolled his eyes. *They are the experts, I guess.* He trotted halfway down the hill until the group found a nice grassy patch where they all could sit together.

The campers encircled the middle of the kickball field. In the middle of the field, Chase and his twin brother were setting up a 12-foot ladder. Mr. Dodd was a large man all around. He trotted over to the ladder and shook it, checking if it was sturdy.

"Seems Secure." Mr. Dodd grumbled. He began climbing the ladder. The ladder shook with every rung he ascended. Every counselor, but Chase and his twin stepped back. They continued to hold the ladder as everyone else backed away in fear the ladder would topple with Mr. Dodd on it.

"Bullhorn!" Mr. Dodd commanded when he reached the

top of the ladder.

The lanky man, Danny had run into minutes before, stepped forward. He stood on his tiptoes as he handed Mr. Dodd a bullhorn. It took Mr. Dodd a few attempts to reach the bullhorn. On his fourth attempt, he finally held the bullhorn in his hand.

Pressing the button Mr. Dodd's voice pierced through the air, "Testing, testing... 1, 2... Bueller, Bueller. Is this thing on?"

All the clammer and commotion around the ladder stopped as nearly everyone covered their ears.

"Can everyone hear me?"

"Yes, Mr. Dodd!" One of the twins shouted. "Everyone can hear you. It's a bullhorn, you don't need to yell!"

"Oh sorry!" Mr. Dodd replied, still using the bullhorn.

"Do you even need the bullhorn?" A camper shouted. Everyone laughed at this.

Mr. Dodd took his finger off the bullhorn's button, "Is this better? Can everyone hear me?"

"Yes!" The campers replied as one.

"Oh great... Here goes his speech." Dez mumbled under her breath.

Guy put his index finger to his lip to indicate quiet.

"Wait, you've been here before?" Danny asked Dez."

Dez copied Guy and motioned quiet because she did not want to answer Danny's question.

"Welcome campers to Camp Fable, where every story has a moral!"

"Yawn!" Dez pretended to yawn by patting her mouth.

"Dez, quiet," Guy whispered.

"For those of you who don't know me, my name is Mr. Dodd, and over by the mess hall is my lovely wife, Mrs. Dodd, we are the Camp Directors." Mr. Dodd pointed towards the mess hall. "To my right is my right-hand man, Mr. Kirby." Mr. Dodd paused, expecting the kids to laugh at his name. When no one, but himself and Mr. Kirby laughed, Mr. Dodd started speaking again. "Mr. Kirby is the Camp Coordinator."

"Wait for it," Dez whispered in Danny's direction.

"Around us, are your camp counselors." Mr. Dodd indicated by waving his hands around frantically, causing the ladder to shake. Chase and his brother held tight, ensuring it wouldn't fall. Everyone else backed away from the ladder snickering as they did. You could tell people were afraid, at any moment Mr. Dodd could tumble from the ladder and no one wanted to be flattened like a pancake.

Mr. Dodd realized how much the ladder was swaying and abruptly stopped waving his hands. He grasped the top of the ladder firmly. Campers started roaring with laughter.

Dez leaned towards Danny. "See, like clockwork... So predictable. You know I've seen him fall twice when giving this speech."

Guy shot her a glare. Dez brushed it off and turned her attention back to Mr. Dodd. Mr. Dodd rather than yelling just waited until the laughter stopped.

"That was a close one." He chuckled to himself. "The

camp counselors are experienced campers themselves and I would suggest that you get to know them well. Now, gentlemen, your cabins are down the path to the left of the mess hall. Ladies, your cabins are to the right of the mess hall. At this time we are going to disperse. Gentlemen, you'll follow your camp counselors down your beaten path and ladies, please follow your counselors to your cabins."

With that, Mr. Dodd began to descend the ladder. Chase's brother held the ladder still as Mr. Kirby and Chase tried their best to help Mr. Dodd down the ladder. To no avail though Mr. Dodd stumbled down the last two rungs and rolled backward, landing on his butt.

He jumped up as quickly as he could, acting as if nothing had happened. Everyone saw, campers tried to hold in snickers. Mr. Dodd looked around trying to hide his frustration with a smile.

Guy turned to the group. "See nothing to worry about. We've done this before Danny. Good to know you're alert."

"Don't you think we should let Mr. and Mrs. Dodd know the campers are in danger?" Danny said frantically, as he followed Guy and Dez.

"Ha! Mr. and Mrs. Dodd? Yeah, they'd be a big help." Dez retorted.

"Hey, where are we headed? Shouldn't we head to our cabin and Dez go to hers?"

"We, Dez and I, are going to go down near the water. You and Ozzie though should head to the cabin. It'll probably be the safest place. Dez and I will let you know if we need you," Guy said as he continued trotting towards the water.

Danny ran in front of Guy and stopped him. "Wait, I thought you said not to go near the water."

Dez walked up to Danny. "We told you not to go near the water, Poindexter. Don't worry about Guy and me."

"Thanks for the concern, Danny, but as Dez said, we've got this. Just stay put in the cabin. We'll let you know when it's safe to come out."

With that Dez and Guy started walking away, leaving Ozzie and Danny to head to the cabin themselves.

"Bunch of loons." Ozzie patted Danny on the shoulder. "Come on, let's go."

Danny did not budge. He pondered on whether he should race after them or just wait in the cabin with Ozzie. Danny decided on going with them. He wanted to experience this world for himself. Not just reality, but fantasy too. In addition, Danny did not like the idea of being left with Ozzie to defend themselves. Guy and Dez were his only hope of staying safe, if anything he was going to stay with them.

"Hey!" Danny charged through the woods and onto the beach.

Ozzie looked around. He did not believe the three of them, but he, like Danny, certainly did not want to be left alone. "Danny, wait!"

Danny caught up to Guy and Dez. "I'm coming with

you."

"Me too." Ozzie said, sliding in next to Danny.

"Poindexter, you're just going to slow us down and Ozzie, you don't even believe any of this. Why would either of you want to come?" Dez snarked at the two of them.

"Woah, woah, woah… Hold up Dez. They may not be trained up in all this, but at least they'd be good lookouts."

Danny nodded in agreement.

"Please!" If there is any truth to what you're saying, I do not want to be alone in that cabin. Especially since I don't have any video games on hand." Ozzie vocalized.

Dez looked at Guy. "Fine, you're editor and chief. It's your call."

"Okay, you two," Guy said. "Do what I say, got it! That includes going back to the cabin if I tell you."

Danny and Ozzie nodded, signifying they understood.

"Okay, let's go and stay close to where the forest meets the beach."

Clouds began to roll in as they formed a line. Guy led the pack, followed by Ozzie, then Danny, and finally Dez bringing up the rear for protection.

"What exactly are we looking for?" Danny asked.

"Non-human footprints on shore, slime, air bubbles in the middle of the lake. You know anything that looks out of the ordinary." Guy said, nonchalantly.

"You mean like this?"

The group turned towards Ozzie, who was holding up a

stick with slim dripping from the end of it.

"Yes, Ozzie like that," Dez replied.

"What is it?" Ozzie asked.

"Looks like snakeskin, but slimier," Danny answered.

"Oh, it's skin alright. It just doesn't belong to a snake. A Water Orc must have shape-shifted into someone. When they do, they shed their skin." Guy stated.

"Nothing to worry about. It's just one skin." Dez said.

"Still gross." Ozzie dropped the stick he was holding. When he did, he jumped back and screamed. "Guys… Do you see what I see?" Pointing to the ground.

Everyone's shift their focus to the ground they were standing on. At first, Danny had just thought the ground was littered with moss. Upon closer examination, he realized the ground was covered in slime.

"What the?!" Gasped Danny.

"Okay, that may be a cause for concern," Dez said.

"What do we do?" Danny was frightened.

"Back to the cabin!" Guy bolted towards Cabin 6.

Raindrops sprinkled from above.

Danny and everyone else followed in tow. What else were they to do, but listen to Guy and Dez? They were the experts, but the cabin? How was that place going to protect them? The door didn't even fully shut.

Guy made it to the cabin door first and flung himself at it. The rest of them followed with Ozzie bringing up the rear. With everyone in, Ozzie slammed the door shut and braced himself up against it.

"What do we do?" Danny repeated as he braced himself up against the door with Ozzie.

"Give me a minute." Guy ran towards the duffle bag he had brought. He stuck his head into the bag.

Danny looked over in amazement. "That is a goblin bag!"

"Standard issue for all at the school newspaper." Dez beamed.

Guy pulled his head out of the bag appearing with three steel hammers. He tossed one to Dez. "Start reinforcing everything."

Dez caught the hammer and immediately swung it at the door that Danny and Ozzie were leaning on. The door magically popped into place and fit the door frame perfectly. She swung the hammer again, this time at the doorknob. It too straightened itself out. Reaching down she flicked the locket shut. One last tap against the door with the hammer and a deadbolt appeared. Dez turned this too to the lock position.

Guy was on the floor hammering away. With every hit, the boards on the floor snapped back into place. He stopped long enough to throw Danny the third hammer he had been holding.

Danny moved out of the way of the hammer. It landed right where he was standing, and the floorboard straightened out. He picked up the hammer, reading along the handle. *Property of Bubba Pig.*

Wow, Danny mouthed. *Is this really from the three little pigs' fairytale?*

"Hey Poindexter, less gawking, more swinging," Dez yelled from up top a beam. Dez was walking across the beam and hammering along the ceiling as she went.

"Right!" Danny sized up a wall. He wound up hitting the wall with everything he had.

There was a *boom* and Danny flew back from the wall.

"Danny, no need to wind up when you're striking something. We're trying to reinforce the cabin, not create more entryways for the Water Orcs." Guy laughed.

"Got it!" Danny got back up and started hitting the walls between the boards without winding up. The boards began to fall into place. "Hey Ozzie, this is fun. You want to give it a try?"

No reply.

Danny looked around the room, "Ozzie?"

It was dark and hard to see now, the clouds were covering all of camp and the rain had picked up. The light from the glass wall that had lit up the entire cabin earlier was no more.

"Ozzie? Ozzie?" Danny continued to look around the room.

Then he spotted him or at least where he was hiding.

There, Ozzie was sitting on one of the bunk beds, under the sheets. Danny could tell this was too much for Ozzie. Ozzie had probably never experienced anything like this. Truthfully, neither had Danny. The only thing he had experienced was the locket that hung around his neck and that, according to Pappy, was only the tip of the iceberg of the world Danny was learning about. He could only imagine what going toe to toe with a Water Orc was going to be like.

Danny shivered at the thought of seeing one. He had only heard about them from Pappy. The last time Pappy met up with a Water Orc, his friend, Buzz, ended up in a wheelchair. Imagine what they would do to Danny and his friends. Danny shook his head getting rid of the thought and turned his attention back to the cabin walls.

"All good up here!" Dez used her acrobatics and the corner of two walls to make her way back to the ground.

"Almost done with the walls," Danny declared, hammering on the last wall.

"Floors are good too. Looks like the only wall left is this glass wall. Either of you want to take a crack at it?" Guy asked.

"Definitely, not Poindexter," Dez chuckled. "He almost knocked down that whole wall with his first hit."

Danny faced the glass wall, "Does it even need to be reinforced? Doesn't look like it is chipped anywhere."

"It may not be chipped, but a few good taps to the glass wall and the glass will thicken. That is how it becomes reinforced." Guy said.

"Well, I vote for you or Dez because I don't want to be blamed for cracking the glass. I don't even know my own strength," Danny said, cracking a smile.

Neither Guy nor Dez smiled at this.

"Whatever. I'll do it." Dez smirked.

Dez pivoted to face the glass wall. Grasped her hammer firmly. She was about to swing, when *crack*. The darkness around them lit up from a bolt of lightning. For a split second, you could see everything outside.

"Did you see that?" Dez asked.

"What, you mean, all the campers on the beach?" Danny said shakily. "They're going to be turned if we don't warn them."

"No Danny, those are already Water Orcs. They've got nearly everyone. If not everyone." Guy shared.

"What?!" Danny yelled. "How can you tell?"

"The footprints in the sand. There are tons and half of them were made by Water Orcs. They got to the campers. We're the only ones left." Guy said.

Danny froze at this news. His face went white. What had he gotten himself into? He was not prepared for any of this. He was downright scared.

Another *crack* and the outside was lit up once again.

"What do we do?" Danny asked. "Radio for backup?"

"We don't even get Wi-Fi here. How do you expect us to make a call out of camp, and in this weather?" Ozzie was still sitting on the bed. His head peeked out from under the covers.

"Hello? Did you not see what we did with these hammers? Guy, you've got to have something in that bag." Danny pleaded.

Guy sat back and thought. As he was thinking, the

outside lit up a third time. This time Dez, who had not taken her eyes off the outside, noticed something.

"Guys!" Dez screamed.

All three of them spun to face Dez.

"What is it?" Guy asked.

"A counselor, look!"

Sure enough, there was Chase running up the beach and to their cabin. As he clambered onto the deck, Danny knew they could not let Chase in. He was convinced Chase was one of the first people who was taken by the Water Orcs, but he could not find the words until it was too late.

Dez opened the sliding glass door. Chase stepped inside the cabin. "Thanks!" He smiled.

Chapter 5

Danny flung himself in front of the others, putting himself between Chase and them. Pulling the hammer above his head Danny told Chase, "Get back! Get back! I'm warning you."

"Danny, what are you doing?" Guy plucked the hammer from Danny's hand before he could hit Chase with it.

"This counselor. Chase. He's one of them." Danny did not back down even without the hammer.

"Poindexter, that's absurd. He's glowing too much to be one," Dez said, flashing Chase a welcoming smile.

"He was one of the first ones to be captured. You said it yourself, the longer a Water Orc is their host's form the more they look and feel normal," Danny replied.

"Are you sure?" Guy asked. Now he was ready to swing the hammers he held at any moment.

"He claims to have a twin!" Danny exclaimed.

Dez too was on alert now. Her welcoming smile quickly faded from her face as she stepped in front of Danny.

Raising her hammer, "Is this true?"

"Woah, woah, woah," Chase jumped back. I just got away from those Water Orcs and now you're accusing me of being one."

"Wait, you know what they are?" Guy asked confusingly.

"Well of course I--"

"Hold on. It's basically pitch black everywhere and you're still wearing your aviators?" Dez questioned.

Chase slumped back. Now he was afraid of them.

"Take them off!" Dez commanded.

Chase stared at her, "Really?"

"I said, take them off," Dez repeated.

"Fine," Chase slowly pulled his sunglasses off. "Are you happy?" Just as he said that his eyelids blinked shut from side to side.

"Holy cow!" Danny screamed as he jumped back. "See I knew it, I knew it. Give me my hammer."

Dez lunged at Chase.

Chase jumped back and caught Dez's hammer mid swing. He used her own momentum to pull Dez along with the hammer and then wrapped his arms around her tight. She was trapped.

"Let her go!" Guy hollered.

"I'm not going to hurt her… Just listen, please… I'm not a Water Orc."

"How do you explain your eyelids then?" Danny asked.

"Ever hear of Atlantis?"

"Yeah, we know about Atlantis. That's where Water Orcs come from, so you're not helping your case buddy" Guy jeered.

"Ha shows how much you know. They don't come from Atlantis; they just want to take it over." Chase's eyelids blinked sideways again. Then they blinked up and down as they normally should.

"What's happening?" Danny asked.

"I just got out of the water. I'm still shifting back to my landform. Give me a second to get my bearings straight."

"So, you do admit it. You are a shapeshifter." Ozzie bellowed. He had not left the bed from which he crawled onto when they entered the cabin.

"I am an Atlantean! Of course, we shapeshift when we come on land." Chase was frustrated. "Wow, my brother Connor is right, you Homo sapiens are not the brightest bulbs in the box."

"Hold up, you actually have a brother?" Guy asked.

"Yeah man… He was the one holding the ladder with me earlier. At least I think that was him. Not really sure when they got him." Chase said, easing the hold he had on Dez.

"They got him, and I don't know what to do. He's the smart one. Me, I just got all the looks and the better personality." Chase joked; tears began to well up in his eyes.

"Why were you still out there if you knew they were all Water Orcs?" Guy asked.

"I didn't know they were all Water Orcs. I didn't even know Connor was one until we got to our submarine."

"What happened when you got to the submarine?" Dez asked.

Chase had let go of Dez and she was now consoling him.

"When we got on to our submarine that's when Connor started acting weird. First, he went to the controls and opened the bay doors. Water Orc after Water Orc boarded the submarine. We were facing them, with Connor behind me. Then he shoved me right into the creatures, I fell on top of a group of them. They grabbed me, but I was able to swim out of the submarine and on to shore.

When the sky lit up, I saw the cabin and made a run here. Luckily you guys were here. I just didn't think you'd be so hostile."

"Sorry if we're a little hostile, but if you haven't looked around, we're surrounded by Water Orcs! Everyone out-" Danny was caught off by Guy.

"Danny, enough!" Guy shouted.

"What! How are you not freaked out?" Danny fired back.

"We've had worse odds before," Dez stated without an ounce of worry in her voice. "And if we have an Atlantean here, then we're one up on these creatures." Dez flashed another smile at Chase.

Danny caught this, *Does she actually believe this guy?*

"So how many Atlanteans are here?" Guy asked.

"Just Connor and me. A few days ago, Atlantis intercepted a message that some Water Orcs were coming here."

"Do you know why?" Guys asked.

"No, the message never said why they were coming here, just that a group was being sent out. Connor and I were asked to come, do a recon mission, and then report back. We were only expecting two to four at most, but it seems they brought double, maybe triple that number. The two of us can't handle that many alone."

Guy paced the floor, "A pack of a dozen of them? They must be searching for something important if there were that many here to begin with."

"Were you able to radio for back-up?" Dez hoped.

"I was able to connect with my cousin Lexi earlier using a seashell… I just hope she doesn't bring her dad," Chase's eyes went wide as he mentioned the word *dad*.

"Whose her dad?" Dez asked.

Chase's voice shook, "King Atlas."

"Your uncle is King Atlas? Let's hope he comes. Those Water Orcs won't stand a chance then!" Dez pumped her first excitedly.

"No, he can't come." Chase shuttered at the thought of seeing his uncle.

"Wait, hold up. Atlas is real? Not just a book of maps!" Danny shrieked.

"Wrong Atlas, Poindexter, there are actually two. One that holds up the sky and the other is the rightful ruler of

Atlantis. Don't mind Poindexter over here. He's just learning all this stuff." Dez said, not taking her eyes off Chase.

"All, we're getting off topic. Chase, how long until your cousin Lexi gets here?" Guy asked.

"It couldn't be more than a day," Chase replied.

Guy walked up to the glass wall and started hammering it lightly to thicken the glass. He hit the lock to the sliding door and the lock doubled in size. *Click,* went the lock as Guy flicked it shut. Hitting it one more time above the lock a deadbolt appeared. He turned the deadbolt until it clicked into place.

"Okay. Dez and Danny look for any part of the cabin that we have missed and hit it with the hammer. I want this place solid, especially if we're going to be here for the night. Ozzie. Where's Ozzie?" Guy spun around until he saw Ozzie's head poking out from under the covers.

"Ozzie, we need you. Dig through my duffle bag and see if you can find some flashlights and what I have in there for snacks."

"What can I do?" Chase said sheepishly.

"Do you still have that seashell?" Guy asked.

"Unfortunately, I dropped it before I made it up the steps onto the deck." Chase stared out the window. Sure enough at the bottom of the steps you could make the faint outline of what looked like a seashell.

"Hey Ozzie, do you see any running shoes in there?" Guy shouted.

Ozzie, who was waist deep into the bag, rustled around for a bit before popping up. "Are these what you're looking for?"

"Perfect," Guy put out his hands ready to catch them. Ozzie's throw was perfect, and Guy caught the shoes without issue.

"Here put these on." Guy told Chase.

"What are they?" Chase looked at the shoes in bewilderment. They appeared to be too small for Chase and the soles of the shoes were worn, like the rubber had been burned off.

"Listen, just put them on. You won't be wearing them long at all." Guy said.

"Are these things safe?" Chase was getting irritated, but so was Guy.

"They're made by Cobbler Elves. Meaning they don't fall apart easily, and they're enchanted with specific powers. These are made for running."

Chase struggled to put the shoes on one after another. He gave the second shoe one last good pull and the shoe slipped on.

"Wait running?" Chase looked frightened.

"Yep." Guy began unlocking the sliding door. "You're going to get the seashell."

"The beach is littered with Water Orcs walking around as campers!" Chase shrieked.

"Someone's got to get the seashell and you are the one who dropped it, not me. Just try not to run into any trees or rocks." Guy smiled.

"Fair point, man," Chase jumped up from the floor smacking the bottom of his shoes. "I think I'd be better off in my sandals."

"Just start out slow," Guy thrust the sliding door open.

Chase took a few steps out the door, turned to the stairs. *Zoom!* Sand flew into the air leaving a line of shoe prints on the beach. The seashell was still at the bottom of the stairs.

Another *zoom* could be heard, and Chase reappeared on the deck outside the sliding doors. He stepped into the cabin tossing the seashell up and down. "Dude, you weren't kidding about these things. They're a little tight, but with these things on I can run just as fast as I swim. Can I keep these?"

"Sorry man, school property, take them off." Guy ordered.

Chase plopped down onto one of the beds and pulled the shoes off, handing them back to Guy, "What now man?"

"Call your cousin. Get an ETA on when she'll be here." Guy ordered.

"Eye, eye Captain!" Chase saluted Guy.

Chapter 6

"Okay, so I got a hold of Lexi. She said that she should be here by sunrise," Chase tossed Guy the seashell and jumped on to a bed.

"What do we now?" Danny asked.

"We wait," Chase replied.

"Yeah, but what about your brother and the others?" Danny asked.

"Dude, they'll be fine. Connor can handle himself," Chase rolled over onto his side. "Just try and get some shuteye."

"Chase is right Danny. Why don't the four of you try and get some rest. I'll stay up and take the first watch," Guy stated.

Dez and Ozzie crawled into a bed each just as Chase had done. Danny on the other hand put his back up against the wall and slid down to sit across from Guy.

"That's alright. I'm not tired yet. I'll stay up with you for a bit," Danny was hoping he could pick Guy's brain about the locket.

"Suit yourself, but you really should get some sleep. You'll need it in the morning," Guy replied.

The two of them sat there in silence. The rain began to let up and you could see the moon light peek through the clouds a little. Then the clouds parted all together and see all the stars in the night sky could be seen.

Looking out the glass window Danny smiled. The night sky reminded him of being on Buzz's porch with Pappy. How the two had marveled at the constellations and the beauty the sky held.

"Pretty nice out there," Guy stood up. "Almost makes you forget that we are surrounded by Water Orcs."

Danny stood up too, "Yeah, it reminds me of one of the last nights I was with Pappy."

"Pappy, who's Pappy?" Guy's face looked confused.

"Oh sorry, it's what I call Grandpa… I know it's silly."

"No, no not at all. I call my grandpa, Gramps."

Danny couldn't help but laugh at this.

"What's so funny?" Now Guy was more confused.

"Oh, nothing... I tried calling Pappy, Gramps once. He was not fond of it. Fired back with, *it's Pappy*," Danny did his best imitation of Pappy.

They both laughed at this.

"You know outside of this fantasy being more real than we're taught, you and your mom were all Mr. Dailey talked about."

Danny quit laughing, "Really?"

"Yeah, you two are his whole world."

"Yeah? That's why he always had that locket on him."

Danny's stomach sank at the mention of Pappy's love for his family. Oh, how he missed Pappy. How he wished that he believed him sooner about all this. Maybe that would have allowed Danny to forgive Pappy sooner and rebuild their relationship. Now though, Pappy was gone once again and this time, Danny and his mom had not heard from Pappy for almost a month.

"Hey, Danny?" Guy was trying to get Danny's attention again.

"Yeah?" Danny looked up.

"I've been meaning to ask you, what exactly does that locket do? I mean it must be enchanted too. Why else would he give it to you to keep safe?

"Wait, you mean he never showed any of you?"

"Nope."

Danny's eyes lit up. Finally, something he knew that Guy didn't. Danny slipped the locket off from around his neck. "Here, grab a hold of the chain. Make sure you hold on tight."

"Why, what's going to happen?"

"Don't worry, nothing bad. It's actually really cool." Danny said with excitement.

Guy reached out and grabbed the chain, holding on tight just as Danny instructed. Good thing too, because just like at Buzz's house on Danny's rite of passage with Pappy, the locket pulled them forward. Guy was startled but held on tight.

Danny looked at Guy with amusement, he wondered if this is how he had looked the first time he had used the locket with Pappy. Then the pulling sensation came to a sudden halt. Danny and Guy now stood in Danny's house.

Guy stood there in awe, taking everything in. *Where am I?* He thought.

As though Danny had read his mind, he said, "We're in my house. My mom is packing for a business trip to China."

"Wow, this is incredible!" Guy craned his neck every which way to get a good look at everything. "Are we really at your house?

"Yeah." Danny smiled.

"Can anyone see us?"

"No, I don't think so. It would be pretty cool if people could see us. I think it's like an out-of-body experience."

"This is so cool."

"Get ready." Danny looked in his mother's direction and was about to let go of the necklace when his mom turned around. Then back to the kitchen refrigerator, she opened it and grabbed a sports drink. She turned back around, now she was heading in Danny and Guy's direction. Rather than walking right past Danny, she stopped in front of him.

Could she see them? Was Guy right in thinking they were there and not just there subconsciously? Danny ached for a hug in that moment from her. He just wanted to be held, to know everything would be alright.

Just when Danny was getting hopeful and about to lean in for a hug... She took another step towards Danny... This was it, she could see him... Danny wrapped his right arms around his mom... His arms went right through her. His mom took a step forward, walking through Danny. Danny turned around realizing he was invisible, watching his mom walk out of the kitchen and down the hallway out of sight. Guy had gotten Danny's hopes up.

Danny sighed, "Ready?"

"Yeah. For wh-?"

Guy did not get a chance to finish his question as Danny let go of the locket and the two of them were pulled back. To Guy, it felt like he was falling, being pulled backward. Then it stopped. Danny and he were back in the cabin with the glow of the moonlight flooding into the room.

"Wow," Guy said under his breath.

"Yeah... Pretty incredible," Danny said with excitement.

Guy slumped back down onto the wood floor, "So you said, you can't see Mr. Dailey?"

"Nope, no luck," Danny's excitement faded as he was reminded, he still did not know where Pappy was.

"Interesting…" Guy was taking everything in. He had never experienced anything like this locket before.

"So do you have any ideas on what this might be?" Danny asked hopefully.

"No, not off the top of my head," Guy said, examining the locket closer. He opened it up and inside the locket was a picture of Danny with his parents in one photo and his grandma in the other. He handed Danny back the locket. "But I'll let you know if I think of anything."

Danny looked defeated at this news. He figured if anyone knew how this locket worked, it would be Guy. Unfortunately, so far, it was another dead end. Danny tucked the locket under his shirt once again for safe keeping.

"Hey Danny, so where is Mr. Dailey?"

Danny sighed. He had been dreading this question. He knew Guy would eventually ask him and still had no clue how to answer him. Should he tell him that he had made a wish with a leprechaun coin for Pappy to disappear altogether? Or should he tell him Pappy was called away on a trip? Neither were lies, but one made Danny sound like he had no fault in Pappy being gone.

"Truthfully. He's off helping a friend, Hank… Though I'm not sure exactly where that is, and I feel partially to blame." Danny looked towards the ground ashamed of the wish he made with the leprechaun coin.

"Why's that?" Guy asked.

"Well, a few days before Pappy set out to help Hank, I made a wish for him to disappear."

Guy laughed at this.

"The wish was with a leprechaun coin." Dainty shared, still looking at the ground. He could not make eye contact with Guy. He barely knew Guy but Danny did care if what Guy thought about him.

"Oh… *Oh,*" Guy said, surprised at this news. He knew if

Danny had wished Mr. Dailey to disappear with a leprechaun coin, then he was good as gone. Then Guy thought, *disappearing could mean a lot of things.* He decided to dig a little.

"So, when you made the wish, how exactly did you word it?" Guy asked, figuring there may be some wiggle room in how Danny worded the wish.

Danny closed his eyes and tried to recall his exact words.

"Think Danny, make sure you tell me the exact wish."

"My exact thought was, I wish Grandpa would just disappear from our lives... forever," Danny opened his eyes.

Guy leaned back against the foot of the bed. How Danny had worded his wish hit Guy like a ton of bricks. "That is pretty specific." Guy knew though, if anyone had a chance to beat the odds for a leprechaun coin, then it would be Mr. Dailey.

Danny dropped his gaze to the floor.

"I wouldn't count Mr. Dailey out yet though. He's been dealt worse odds before."

"Really?" Danny asked hopefully.

"Of course, I mean look at what we are dealing with. This is a lot, but Dez and I have seen worse before. We'll get through this and I'm sure Mr. Dailey will be back by the start of school."

Danny turned his attention to the outside. He could see the beach was littered with Water Orcs who had shifted into campers. The creatures had, yet to realize Danny and his friends were inside the cabin, unchanged, still in their original forms.

"I still don't see how we're going to get out of this… I'm not made for this like you and Dez."

Guy laughed, "No one's made for this. You just have to believe in yourself."

"Huh?"

"You know, like Jack and the Beanstalk?"

"Yeah, I know the story of Jack and the Beanstalk." Danny replied.

"Then you know Jack had insurmountable odds to defeat the giant and claim the Golden Goose, but he didn't give up."

"He didn't?"

"No, he climbed that beanstalk, grabbed the Golden Goose, and defeated the giant. He did this all by believing in himself."

"Yeah, but that is just a-" Danny stopped himself.

"Just a story? Come on Danny, look around us. You still think stories are just all fantasy. No, they're not and the real Jack certainly did not have a chance to practice fighting a giant. He just trusted in himself, and he won." Guy exclaimed.

"Trust in myself," Danny mumbled. He sat back and gave it a thought. Danny just needed to believe in his abilities a little and things would go right. Besides, he had four friends on his side. *Well, two*, he thought. He was not too sure how much help Ozzie and Chase would truly be.

"Are you just saying all this to make me feel better?" Danny found himself asking louder than he wanted to.

"You obviously don't know me well enough. Yes, we're safe here. It will be light soon and Chase's cousin will be here with reinforcements. Then we will find where the Water Orcs are storing the campers."

"What do you mean?"

"Well, when a Water Orc shapeshifts into someone then they need a cold place to store their host's body, somewhere really cold. This makes it easier for them to stay in the form they acquired."

"Like a cooler?" Danny's voice shook as he asked.

"Yeah, a cooler would work, but you'd need a really big one."

"Like the giant one in the kitchen of the mess hall?"

"Yeah, but I'm not sure if they have one."

"Oh, they do," Danny assured Guy. "When everyone else exited the mess hall from the front I tried escaping through the back of the kitchen. Almost made it until I ran into Mr. Kirby."

Guy laughed at this, "Ah, Mr. Kirby. He's a great guy. A little scary, but he means well."

"Wait, you know him?" Danny was confused. *Has Guy been to camp before, just like Dez?*

"Of course, I know him. So does Dez too. He's the head custodian at Meadowbrook High." Guy laughed.

"Huh, really?"

"Yep. Mr. and Mrs. Dodd are our vice principal and principal."

Well, would you look at that? Danny thought.

"So do they all know about the school newspaper?" Danny asked.

"Oh no... Well, they know there's a school newspaper. They just don't know what our true purpose is." Guy smirked,

"Well, who does?"

"As far as teachers. Just Mr. Dailey."

Danny thought about this for a moment. So Pappy, Danny, Guy, Dez, and now Ozzie were the only ones at the school who knew the truth about what evil lies out there. He did not know if he should be honored or horrified at this revelation.

Guy could see the look on Danny's face. "Don't worry there are more reporters back at school. We're not the only ones trying to keep the world in balance." Guy said with a grin.

Whew, that's a relief, Danny thought.

"Take my advice Danny, get some sleep. You're going to need your strength." Guy said as he pulled in the curtains a little more to cover up the moonlight. "I'll keep watch and get you if anything happens."

Danny nodded. Now that Guy had mentioned it, sleep did sound really good. Danny picked up the hammer that belonged to Bubba Pig and slowly walked to the empty bed. Crawling under the covers he held the hammer tight as though he was five again and the hammer was his security blanket. He did not know how effective the hammer would be against the creatures, but figured it was better than nothing.

Chapter 7

Within minutes Danny found himself asleep, dreaming. He was in the cabin, but this time it was empty. All his friends were gone, and the cabin was still surrounded by Water Orcs. His heart raced, what was he going to do? Danny took a step back. He bumped into someone.

Dez! He thought, spinning around.

It wasn't Dez this time, "Pappy!" Danny shouted as he hugged him tightly.

"Danny Boy! Pappy wrapped his arms around Danny.

Danny looked up at Pappy, "Where are you?"

"Kind of in a pickle, but it appears you are too." Pappy walked to the edge of the cabin and peered outside the glass wall. He chuckled seeing all the Water Orcs.

"How do I get us out of this? This is too much!"

"Oh, come on, this is nothing." Pappy turned back to Danny.

"Easy for you to say, I've never been in a situation like this before."

"Do you think any of us were actually ready for this when we first started?"

"Oh, come on Pappy, that's not fair. You're a legend." Danny stepped back from Pappy.

Pappy smiled and chuckled at this. "Listen, I may be the exception, but do you think Guy or Dez were ready their first time?"

"They may not have been ready, but at least they had you!" Danny grumbled.

"And you have them. Those two are some of the best reporters I've ever had at the newspaper."

"Yes, they're great. Though they're not you. Can you at least tell me where you are?"

"Would you believe me if I told you?"

"Try me," Danny replied.

Pappy chuckled, "A whole other world."

Danny laughed. "Another world?"

"Yep," Pappy smiled. "It's a new one for me too."

"Where is this other world?"

Pappy put a hand on Danny's shoulder, "Don't you worry Danny Boy, I'll be home soon enough. Just remember, Jack and the Beanstalk. Believe in yourself."

Danny started hearing shrieks from all around. He wrapped his arms around Pappy as tight as he could. It felt as though Pappy was really here, that this was not just a dream.

The shrieks got louder.

Pappy leaned over and whispered, "Jack and the

Beanstalk."

With that Danny woke. *Jack and the Beanstalk. Jack and the Beanstalk.* he thought, sitting up in bed.

Thud, thud. Every part of the cabin shook as Water Orcs shrieked and banged on the glass wall. With every hit from the creatures a new crack formed along the wall.

Guy was already at the wall frantically pounding away with his hammer. "Danny! Dez! I could really use your help here!"

Dez was halfway across the room while Danny was still trying to get his bearings straight. Focusing, Danny was prepared to help reinforce the wall. He stood up and looked for the hammer. He could not see where it was. He pulled the sheets off the bed and the hammer flew on to the floor. Scooping it up he headed to join Guy and Dez.

"Go reinforce the main door. We've got everything here." Dez said as another crack formed in the wall.

Danny was not too sure if they had the wall secured, but who was he to argue? He ran over to the front door of the cabin, just as the lock started to splinter. The door banged in and out a few times until it flew open.

There stood a Water Orc, unchanged, right in front of Danny. Slime oozed off the Water Orc as it stepped further into the cabin. It left a wet footprint with every step.

Danny froze from shock, not knowing what to do. Slime flew off the creature as it flailed its arms reaching for Danny. The Water Orc was about to close in when out of nowhere Chase rammed into it with all his might, pushing it out the door.

"Quick!" Chase slammed the door shut. "Hammer away!"

Danny was frozen in place as his brain was still trying to process what just happened. He was centimeters from a Water Orc. *What would have happened if the creature had touched me?* Danny wondered.

"Danny, get the door!" Chase yelled as the cabin door he leaned on continued to bang in and out.

Danny snapped back to reality and ran towards the door, hammer in hand and began pounding away.

"Here." Chase pointed to a spot as Danny began to slow. "And here… One last one, here."

Gradually the banging on the door stopped. The creature must have given up because the door was too sturdy now. Then the thumping on the windows lessened too. The Water Orcs receded back towards the beach.

"What are they doing?" Dez asked.

Chase ran towards the glass wall. "It looks like they're regrouping."

"Regrouping, why?" Danny asked panicked.

"I don't know why. Create a better plan of attack?" Chase guessed.

"That, that was an actual Water Orc," Ozzie stammered.

"Yes Ozzie, we know." Dez rolled her eyes. "You're just now getting this?"

"No, I mean that Water Orc hadn't shapeshifted." Ozzie declared.

"They must be starting to multiply." Chase replied.

"Multiply?" Danny had forgotten that the Water Orcs could multiply.

"Yeah, multiply. As in one can become two. It happens when a Water Orc has gained all its host's memories. The second Water Orc can now take over another host." Chase stated, as though this was common sense.

"Right…" Ozzie said, hesitantly. "So how are we going to get out of this?"

"How far is Lexi from here?" Asked Guy.

"I don't know, let me check." Chase walked back towards the bed, picked up the seashell and began speaking into it.

Danny listened closely. He could hear Chase talking, but he didn't hear any sound on the other end.

"Hey, are any of you listening to his conversation?" Danny asked out the side of his mouth.

"You mean lack thereof." Dez replied.

"Yeah, I hear it too, or at least what's missing." Guys whispered back.

Although Chase was talking into the seashell, no one was replying on the other end. This was weird to the group. Then it clicked, this was not Chase, it was a Water Orc; Fake Chase. The real Chase had been captured just like Connor.

"Why did he save me from the one that just burst through the door then?" Danny asked shakily.

"Not too sure why Poindexter, my guess is he was sent

here to keep an eye on us." Dez said in a hushed voice.

"Yeah, he must be stalling until they find what they're looking for." Guy said.

"What do you mean, what are they looking for?" Danny asked more confused than ever.

"Argh! This kid, can't he keep up?" Dez asked, irritated. "Poindexter haven't you stopped to think, why are they here?"

Danny replied, "Yeah, I have. I mean I figured they're looking for something, but does that really matter?"

Dez gave another groan. She wondered how much more of Danny she could take. Pappy had made Danny out to be this wonder kid, when really, he was just like every other kid starting out in the newspaper; green.

"Danny, yes, it's important. Water orcs just don't attack humans out of anywhere. They were sent here for a reason. You guys distract him." Guy said. "I'm going to make a run for the mess hall with the speed shoes. I'm sure the real Chase is in the kitchen cooler. He'll know what to do."

"What if he makes a move?" Danny pleaded.

"He won't, he's just stalling, so the Water Orcs can accomplish what they were sent here to do." Dez stated.

Just then Chase came up from behind the group. "So, you guys figured it out?"

The group spun around and faced Fake Chase.

Guy made a dive for the speed shoes. As he did though Fake Chase tackled him and multiplied. There in the cabin stood Fake Chase and now another one.

The second Water Orc grabbed Guy who was still reaching for the speed shoes. Guy began to slowly freeze from the Water Orc's touch. Once Guy was fully frozen the Water Orc began changing into Guy.

First, he shifted into the shape of Guy, then his skin shed off, and finally, the Water Orc started moving its new arms and legs.

"Freaky!" Ozzie mouthed.

The only noticeable difference between Guy and the Water Orc, who had just transformed into him, was that New Guy was eerily pale. It was like he had never been in the sun.

"Danny!" Dez shouted, "The shoes!"

The speed shoes were right at Danny's feet. He was about to slide them over to Dez when Fake Chase grabbed her. New Guy grabbed Ozzie.

"You're not going anywhere!" Fake Chase, yelled to the group.

"Danny run!" Dez commanded. "Go find help!"

Danny stood there not knowing what to do.

Dez broke free from Fake Chase's grasp and picked up a hammer. "Go, I've got this!" Dez swung the hammer connecting with the New Guy who was holding Ozzie. New Guy stumbled back and released Ozzie.

Ozzie ran to the goblin bag. "Danny, listen to Dez!"

Danny, still frozen, was unsure if he could do it. If he'd be able to go find help out there, among all the Water Orcs. Then he thought of the story Guy had just told him, and the dream he had with Pappy in it. They both mentioned Jack and the Beanstalk and the moral of it. *Just trust in myself,* he thought.

Ozzie yelled again, "Here take this!" Ozzie threw a hard hat with a headlamp on it to Danny. The hard hat had come from the goblin bag when Guy told Ozzie to find them flashlights and snacks.

Danny slid the shoes on, not bothering to tie them. Looking out at the beach it was dotted with Water Orcs that were multiplying off from their shapeshifted form. He turned the light on from the hard hat and opened the sliding door.

He stretched his toes standing on the cabin deck. Examining the beach and the path to the mess hall before he took off, Danny knew he already regretted stepping outside.

At the bottom of the staircase Danny saw a Water Orc approaching. Knowing he had to move fast Danny put one foot in front of the other and took off. *Zoom!*

Danny was going too fast to notice just how much momentum he had. He plowed into the Water Orc and sent it flying. All along Danny was doing his best not to trip over anything.

Danny soared off the trail and past the mess hall. By the time realized he had passed the mess hall Danny was already by the girls' cabins. *Oh no, this is bad, this is really bad.*

"Shoot!" He yelled, trying to come to a complete stop

before running into the side of a mountain. Danny slid to a stop as best as he could before tripping over the shoelaces he had not tied earlier. He toppled onto his hands and knees, landing inches away from the bottom of the mountain.

Standing up Danny brushed himself off. *What am I doing? I shouldn't be here!* He bent down and began tying the shoelaces. Just then Danny heard a shriek. He wasn't sure if it was a Water Orc or one of his friends.

He took a minute before gaining the courage to make another try and get inside the mess hall. Gingerly, Danny took a step forward, then another and another, and he was off. This time, though, he was only at a quarter of the speed as before.

It was still faster than he could run, but at least at this speed he could stay on the path and choose which direction he was running. Coming to the center of camp Danny followed the path to the mess hall. As he approached the mess hall he began to decelerate.

He pushed the mess hall door open and was inside. The room was dark and empty. Luckily, the hard hat he had illuminated his path to the kitchen. Getting closer Danny could hear some rustling of pots and pans.

It must be Water Orcs, Danny thought. *How many are there though?*

Danny peeked through the plastic window in the swinging door. His light landed right where the sound was coming from. Two Water Orcs spun their heads in his direction. He ducked and flicked the light off.

Did they see me? Danny wondered.

Gazing through the plastic window Danny saw the creatures heading to the kitchen door. He ducked out of sight once again. Thinking, he recognized his best bet would be to charge them.

He waited for them to get closer. With each step they took the *thuds* became louder. Danny took a few steps back and got into a running pose. *Jack and the Beanstalk, Jack and the Beanstalk!*

The kitchen door swung a few centimeters. The Water Orcs were lined up. Danny charged forward at what he thought was quarter speed.

Smack! Danny hit the swinging door.

He burst through the door and into the creatures with more force than he wanted. Both of them flew through the air and smashed into rolling tables filled with pots and pans. The hit knocked the Water Orcs unconscious.

"Yes!" Danny shouted before he realized where he was.

Quickly, he ducked down hiding behind the nearest rolling table. He flicked his head lamp back on and searched for the wall with the cooler. He spotted it.

Now I just have to make my way over there, he thought.

On his hands and knees, Danny crawled to the cooler door, reaching it with no problems. Pulling the door open he was hit with a blast of frigid air.

Wow, that's cold. He thought as he stepped into the cooler letting the door shut behind him. Once the door shut the cooler lights came on and Danny's jaw dropped.

There, stacked on top of each other along the walls, was over half the camp including Mr. and Mrs. Dodd. He walked past the frozen campers keeping an eye out for Chase. After what felt like forever his eyes fell on a counselor that looked exactly like Chase.

Danny glanced at the name tag. It did not read Chase, but rather another familiar name, Connor. He pivoted around to see if he could find Chase, but with no luck could not see him.

At least I found one of the brothers, thought Danny.

Danny put his hands on Connor and immediately removed them. Connor's body was freezing. How was Danny going to get him out of here? Better question, how was he going to get Connor thawed?

Right when Danny was starting to doubt himself, he saw the solution. Pushed to the back of the cooler was a dolly cart. He had never used one before but figured it could not be that hard to use. All he had to do was get Connor onto the dolly and then he could wheel him out. How he was going to get him thawed he was unsure.

One thing at a time, Danny thought.

Danny brought the dolly up next to Connor. He wobbled Connor back and forth like a block of ice until Connor was standing on the dolly. Danny tilted the dolly back and pushed forward with all his might. With the help of the speed shoes, the dolly moved forward. The cooler door pushed open and the two of them were out.

As Danny wheeled Connor around the kitchen, he spotted it; the answer to how he was going to thaw Connor out. Rushing towards the stoves he turned on the ovens cranking up the heat and opening up the oven doors.

Please be the right choice, please be the right choice. Danny stood guard next to Connor. Minutes ticked away and slowly Connor's color started to come back. Then Danny heard it. The slow drip of water.

Connor let out a, "Woah… Wow! Now that is cold." Connor looked around the room. "Where am I?"

"You're in the mess hall kitchen," Danny stated.

Connor, still a little frozen, turned his head to Danny. "How long was I out? Better question: who are you?"

"Not sure how long you were in there, but I'm Danny."

Connor's face turned white. "Oh shoot, did my uncle send you?" He began to squirm like he was trying to get his legs to work.

Danny smiled at this, "No, I'm just a camper. I was looking for your brother but found you instead."

"Chase, you know Chase? Where is he?" Connor asked frantically, able to move his legs finally. He stepped off the dolly.

"Not exactly, but I know a Water Orc who is masquerading as him."

"They got him too?"

"Yeah, my friends are back at my cabin with him."

"You and your friends caught a Water Orc?"

"Well, not exactly," Danny replied.

"You, a bunch of Homo sapiens caught a Water Orc?"

"No, we didn't. He actually fooled us into thinking he was Chase. That was until we realized he never called your cousin Lexi. Now he has split into two and has become one of my friends."

Being able to fully move Connor raced over to the windows facing the beach. "Wow, how many are there?"

"Not too sure, but enough that we need more than us." Danny began shutting the ovens off and closing the doors.

"How'd you make it past all those Water Orcs?"

"Oh, my friend, Guy, had some speed shoes from Cobbler Elves."

"Ah, gotcha." Connor took notice of the worn out shoes Danny was wearing. "Those are some pretty cool kicks."

"Thanks," Danny replied as Connor scanned the room. "What are you looking for?"

"Where'd you find me?"

Danny pointed towards the cooler, "Oh, you were in the cooler, over there."

Connor flung the cooler door open. "Wow, they really did a number on camp," referring to all the campers housed in the cooler.

Connor examined the cooler for Chase. "I don't see my brother."

"Neither did I. I thought you were him until I read your name tag."

Connor chuckled. "Yeah, that happens a lot. So what's the game plan?"

"Not too sure. I was told to get Chase, well, you in this case. I'm hoping you could tell us what the plan is."

Connor nodded approvingly, "I dig it, follow me." Connor headed to the swinging kitchen door with the expectation that Danny would follow.

"What about the others?" Danny pointed to the cooler. "We can't leave them in there. They are like human popsicles."

"Danny, we can't thaw them out now. If we do, what do we tell them? Hey, you were captured, copied, and frozen… Now your camp is infested with Water Orcs, but don't worry, help is on the way… We hope." Connor said sarcastically.

"Gesh. Alright already, you don't have to be so mean about it."

"Sorry man, it's just my brother is missing, and the Water Orcs have practically cloned everyone. Today is not a good day."

Danny huffed, "It's okay… What's your plan?" He said, walking past Connor and out into the dining room of the mess hall.

"It's simple. You lead me to the cabin. I'll take down the Water Orc who cloned Chase and then I'll radio my cousin, Lexi, on the seashell."

"That sounds like Fake Chase's plan." If Danny had not found Connor frozen, he would have thought he was a Water Orc, just by the fact he had the same plan as Fake Chase.

"Yes, but this time Lexi will actually be called." Connor stopped, putting his arm out in front of Danny. "Hold up." Connor looked outside the mess hall. "How'd you get by the Water Orcs before?"

"I told you," Danny pointed to his feet. "The shoes."

"Oh, right. Well, that may not work for both of us." Connor shifted his gaze up and to the side as though he was thinking. "I got it. Let's creep along as best as we can. If we see any Water Orcs, you can just charge them."

"Good idea, stay off the beach and follow the wooded path. There are more on the beach than in the woods and there is a glass wall facing the beach. If Fake Chase sees you coming, then he won't be so easy to take down."

"Genius Danny, lead the way!" Connor gestured for Danny to pass him.

Chapter 8

Danny and Connor made it quickly to Cabin 6's front door. Danny ended up only having to take out one Water Orc along the way. Surprisingly, he was quite good at operating the speed shoes. Danny wondered if Guy would let him keep them. His guess was not though, Dez would butt in and say, *those are school property,* or something like that.

"Connor, wait here. I'm going to go around the other side and check things out. I'll come back and we can make a plan of attack."

"Why don't I just kick it down?"

Danny laughed, "By all means, you can try, but that cabin is as sturdy as a brick house."

"Huh?"

"Huff and puff all you want, but you won't be blowing this cabin down." Danny laughed even harder.

Connor did not get the reference and just stared blankly at Danny.

"Never mind. Be right back."

Danny crept to the other side of Cabin 6. Glancing through the glass wall he did not see anyone in the cabin. *Dang, it! Did Fake Chase and New Guy get a hold of Dez and Ozzie?*

Not giving up hope, Danny took a deep breath and flung the sliding glass door open. He sped into the room covering every inch of it but found nothing. He was about ready to unlock the front door when he heard a *thud*.

"Don't move." Dez growled from behind. "One more move and I'll clobber you."

Danny's face went white. *They got Dez!* He thought. In one movement Danny slid sideways and behind Dez, hoping to catch the Water Orc off guard.

The Dez-like figure was too quick. Instead of Danny getting the drop on it, the creature swept his legs and he fell right on his back. Before he could do anything, the Water Orc sprang on top of him. The creature and Danny were nose to nose, and it had the upper hand. Danny was about ready to scream for Connor when the Water Orc froze.

"Poindexter!" Dez yelled. "Is that you?"

"Dez?"

Dez and Danny began examining each other. Finally, Dez got off of Danny when she realized his skin was neither cold nor pale. She grabbed his hand and helped him up.

"What happened here?" Where are the others?" Danny questioned.

"Shortly after you left Fake Chase, New Guy, and another Water Orc froze Ozzie. They were about to go after me, so I vaulted to the ceiling and stayed up there. They almost climbed up there but then ended up backing off."

Thud, thud, thud, came from the front door. Connor was still outside. "Danny, you, okay?"

Before Danny could reply Connor yelled again. "Stand back, I'm going to break the door down." The door still did not budge. "Danny, are you okay?"

"Yeah, give me a second." Danny walked to the door, flipped the lock, and turned the knob.

Connor, who was already running, was expecting to collide with the door, but there was no door to hit now. He tumbled into the cabin landing face-first on the wood floor.

Dez let out a big "Ha-ha!"

Danny laughed too, but not as hard.

Connor got off the floor. "You know, I had that."

"I'm sure you did," Dez replied. "So tell me, who are you Chase, Connor, or just another Water Orc?"

"Ha-ha, funny." Connor fired back. "Name's Connor, and you are?"

"I'm Dez. The only one, other than Poindexter here, who has not had a Water Orc double."

"Huh. That surprises me. A whole camp and it's me with two Homo sapiens."

"Hey! Watch yourself there!" Dez yelled. Homo sapiens was seen as a slang term to her. The times she had been called one was to insult her. "It's human."

"Sorry… Human." Connor apologized. "My bad."

"Well, you should be sorry, Poindexter here saved your life."

"Really Dez. Can't we drop the Poindexter?" Danny asked.

Dez smirked, "That's a negative Poindexter."

"Come on, I just risked my life to go get us, Chase."

"Hey, it's Connor." Connor corrected Danny.

"Sorry, Connor. I mean, what have you been doing Dez?"

"Well, when you were out finding Connor, I found out where the Water Orcs are headed. You know the reason they're here."

"Oh really?" Connor asked. "And why are they here?"

"The caves!" Dez announced, spinning towards Connor.

"Yes, we know Water Orcs love caves. They are dark, dreary, and damp. Tell us something we don't know." Connor taunted Dez.

"Two words for you, *trabea punctum*." Dez emphasized the last two words.

Connor turned on his heels and laughed in Dez's face.

Dez just nodded her head slowly as she repeated herself. "Yep. Trabea punctum."

Danny was lost, "Guys, what's *trabea punctum*?"

Connor answered. "Trabea punctum is Latin for shift point. They're legends. Legends are not real."

"That's not true. We haven't come across any." Dez replied.

"Wow, you are a slow Homo sapiens."

"You really want to tango?" Dez said, raising her hammer over her head.

"What do they do? What story are they from?" Danny asked.

"Legends aren't written down." Connor said through gritted teeth. "Without being written down, they cannot exist. The Water Orcs might as well be chasing their own shadows."

Dez let out a big laugh. "Shadows are real! Boy are you slow for an Atlantean. Sure, you're not really a Water Orc?"

"Guys! Focus… Let's say trabea punctums exist. What are they?"

"They're not from any story," Dez replied. "Trabea is Latin for shift and punctum is Latin for point. These shift points were created when reality and fantasy started to mesh."

"For years people and creatures have been searching for them, but none have been found. That's why they are *legends!*" Connor yelled directly into Dez's face.

"Just because one has never been found does not mean they do not exist." Dez fired back, not backing away from Connor. "If they do exist and the Water Orcs find one, then the world is in *big trouble.*"

Connor eased off a little, "Yes, I'll admit. *If* and that is a big *If.* If trabea punctums exist then Dez is right, we are all in trouble, but no legend has ever existed."

Dez's voice rose with every word and every word was clearly directed at Connor. "There was a point in time fairytales, folklore, and mythology did not exist! That stories, were just stories, made up! But hey, an Atlantean is standing right in front of me."

"We have always existed Dez!" Connor fired back.

Danny could tell things were getting heated. He stepped in between Connor and Dez before they got any closer, "Okay, so let's run a hypothetical scenario." Danny said trying to appease Connor.

Connor turned around. "I'm listening."

Dez's posture changed, and she lowered her hammer.

"If trabea punctums exist, what could one do if they found one?" Danny asked.

"Well, *if* they exist, then they could be opened again. By opening one of these shift points again and letting fantasy take over all of human reality. Balance in the world would be lost." Dez stated.

"Balance… That is one thing Pappy, my grandpa, was explaining to me on my rite of passage." Danny stopped and thought, *Is this what Pappy was trying to do with the books? Are the books another trabea punctum?*

"What if I found one? Can trabea punctums be objects?" Danny asked worriedly.

"No, according to legend trabea punctums are only landmarks… well-hidden ones at that," Connor said. "I don't know why we are discussing this though as trabea punctums are not real."

"What are we going to do?" Dez was frustrated with Connor, but they would have to work out their differences later. Then her frustration turned to fright. *What if trabea punctums are real and one is here?* Dez did her best to hide how scared she had just become.

Danny caught on though and sensed Dez was starting to worry. This caused him to sweat and begin doubting himself again. *What do we do, what do we do?... Jack and the Beanstalk, Jack and the Beanstalk... It's not working... Shoot.* His heart began racing.

Connor saw the fear in their eyes. While he was certain legends did not exist, he still knew they had to do something about the Water Orcs. "Okay, let's relax. We must do something about the Water Orcs. I'll just make a call to Atlantis and get some reinforcements."

"How?" Danny asked. His heart slowed a little at hearing that Connor could make a call to Atlantis.

"Well, yeah. I just need a seashell." Connor stated.

Dez walked over to the seashell that Fake Chase had left behind. She picked it up off the bed and tossed it to Connor.

Connor caught the seashell. "Thanks."

"How many Atlanteans do you think you can get here?" Danny asked, hoping they would have an army soon.

"Oh, I could have a whole army here if I wanted to, but we just need one." Connor stated.

"Who's that?" Dez asked.

"My cousin Lexi... Oh, and we should probably find my

brother, Chase." Connor shrugged his shoulders.

"Why does your plan sound eerily similar to the Water Orc's plan?" Dez asked.

"It's quite simple. Water orc's gain a host's memories the longer they have a hold of them. I'm surprised you, being a brilliant *human, didn't* know that." Connor replied.

Connor took the seashell and held it like a cellphone. He blew into the bottom end. As he blew into the shell you could hear Water Orcs shrieking outside. The sound waves skimmed through the water forming ripples that moved from the seashore out to the middle of the lake. The ripples traveled from the lake to the bay and then deep into the ocean.

A groggy voice could be heard on the other end of the seashell "What now?"

"Lexi, it's Connor."

"Connor…" Lexi looked at her watch. "Do you know what time it is? It's not even light out."

"I know… Chase and I kind of ran into a problem up here."

Argh! Not again, Lexi thought. "I knew something would happen. Should I go get my dad now?"

"No, don't do that. Please don't." That was the last thing Connor wanted, to see his uncle, King Atlas. Water orcs he could handle, but his uncle. That was a different story.

"What happened now?" Lexi said, sitting up.

"Well, you know how Chase and I assured you that we could handle the Water Orcs that were attacking that camp full of Homo sapiens?"

Dez gritted her teeth at this.

"You mean humans?" Lexi hated it when he referred to humans as Homo sapiens.

"Yes, sorry, humans."

"That's better." Lexi reached for the glass of water by her bedside table.

Connor took a deep breath. He knew Lexi would not be happy with what he was about to tell her. "Well, now the camp has been overrun by Water Orcs."

Lexi spat the water out, "What?!"

"Yeah, the Water Orcs got the jump on us, but don't worry some more than average humans freed me from the Water Orcs."

Lexi let out a big laugh, "Ha-ha! Would you look at that, Connor the almighty being rescued by some humans? Oh, this I have to see… Wait, where's Chase?"

"That…" Connor hesitated, should he tell her everything? He decided against it, if he told her she would bring her dad then. "That is something we're still trying to figure out." The news Connor was giving Lexi was bad enough without mentioning the trabea punctums. Unlike him, she believed in legends.

"I'm on my way."

"Can you hurry?" Connor's voice shook as he asked the question. "The Water Orcs have already turned the entire camp and I don't know how much longer the cabin's going to hold up."

Lexi began gathering her stuff. "I'll try to grab a cruiser. Just see if you can get a lead on where Chase is."

Lexi hung up the seashell, grabbed her staff, and walked out of her room. She was heading towards the garage when someone turned on a hallway light. Lexi ducked behind the counter as her mother, Basilea, came into view. Keeping the kitchen island between her mother and her, Lexi, still crouching, shuffled to the garage.

Basilea spun around but saw nothing. Lexi had made it to the garage, grabbing keys to a cruiser. She walked over and floated it out the side door before firing it up.

Chapter 9

Back at the cabin Danny stood looking out at the beach. With the sun coming up he could finally see the true chaos that was outside encircling the cabin. Once what was clear sand was no more. Now the beach was muddled with slimy skin, Water Orcs that had shifted into campers, and Water Orcs still in their original form. With every passing minute, it appeared that the number of Water Orcs was doubling.

"This is a bad nightmare, isn't it?" Dez asked.

Danny jumped at this question. He had no clue anyone else was awake. He thought he was the only one up. "Gosh, you scared me."

"Relax Poindexter. It's just me," Dez stood next to Danny. "Hey, I've been meaning to ask you why'd you volunteer to run out there? I mean Guy or I could have easily done it."

"I don't know… I was hoping maybe you would stop calling me Poindexter." Danny said with a smirk.

"Not a chance, Poindexter," Dez winked while saying

Poindexter. "Really though, why'd you, do it? Someone as green as you have never faced anything like this."

"I don't know if someone had to… and well… I didn't want to chance losing one of you… but Guy and Ozzie still got captured. This just reminds me of when Pappy went missing and-"

"Wait, Mr. Dailey is missing? When did this happen?"

"Last month when he took me on a road trip."

"Your rite of passage." Dez interrupted. "Sorry, go on."

"Yes, my rite of passage. How did you know he called it that?"

Dez let out a big, *argh!* "That is all he talked about near the end of last school year. He'd go on and on about how you and he would go on this great road trip. This adventure where he would reveal the real world to you. He was so excited… He believed the two of you would come back from the trip closer than ever, ready to take on the world!"

Dez raised her arm for this next part and moved it from left to right like she was writing the title of a newspaper article. "Danny Boy and Pappy, the defenders of our world. Honorable mention, Scan the School," She let out a laugh as she finished imagining this.

Danny laughed too, though this was due to embarrassment. "Oh gosh... He called me Danny Boy at school?"

"Yes, he did." Dez said pointing and laughing.

"I think I like Poindexter better." Danny replied jokingly.

"Oh, don't worry, Poindexter is sticking." Dez slapped her knee.

Although Danny was scared of what was coming next; battling the Water Orcs and closing the trabea punctum, he was still having fun. He could not remember the last time he had laughed this hard. He got control of his laughter and continued the conversation with Dez.

"So Pappy and I were on my rite of passage when he got a phone call from a friend, Hank," Danny paused. "The call caused us to change our plans and head straight to the University of Iowa where Hank is a professor. By the time we got there though Hank's office had been ran-sacked and only a few clues were left behind on where he may be.

"Right away Pappy and I exited the office. He took me to the nearest airport to put me on a plane home. Pappy insisted the trip was too dangerous for me at that point, and that is when he handed me this."

With that, Danny reached under his shirt and showed Dez his locket. He opened the locket up to reveal two pictures. One of Grandma Yevonne and the other, Danny with his mom and dad.

Dez peered at the locket. She squealed. "Oh, how cute. Little Poindexter with his family."

Feeling embarrassed Danny pulled the locket away and shut it. He turned away from Dez in irritation. He had shown her something that had meaning to him and all she did was laugh.

"Danny, I'm sorry. I didn't mean anything."

"Go away Dez." Danny said, grumpily. He spun around, focusing on the outside. Lexi had to be arriving any minute.

"Really Danny, I didn't mean anything. It's a nice picture of you and your family."

Danny, still facing away from Dez, wiped a tear from his eyes. "It's the last thing Pappy gave me."

"Really Danny, I didn't mean anything by it." Dez stretched out her hand to grab Danny's.

At that moment all Danny wanted to do was get away from there. He wanted to be transported somewhere else. Danny pulled the locket out from under his shirt and thought of his mom. Just before Danny gripped the locket Dez's hand enclosed around Danny's hand.

The two of them were transported out of the cabin and whisked through the air. Further and further, they moved away from the cabin until they found themselves standing on the front porch of Danny's house. Danny's mother sipping a cup of coffee right next to them.

"Where are we?" Dez asked in amazement.

"Shh. Don't let go of my hand." Danny replied. Though he didn't care for Dez to be there he thought maybe being here would show her what the locket means to him. What it meant for Pappy to entrust him with it.

"We're out on the front porch at my house," Danny said.

"Wow, how'd we get here?" Dez whispered.

"It's the locket. It's enchanted."

"Are you able to see Mr. Dailey?"

Danny's eyes sunk at this question and a frown formed.

"Sadly no, I've only dreamt about him."

"What? When did you dream about him?"

"Earlier tonight." Danny smiled.

"What did he say to you? Did he tell you where he was?"

"No, he didn't say exactly. He just said he was in another world."

Dez squealed at this news, "He's in the fantasy world. He must have found a trabea punctum. They do exist!"

"Dez, it was just a dream. He is not in the fantasy world." Though Danny said this, he did not believe his own words. The dream felt real and now knowing there may be a trabea punctum nearby, this could mean Pappy was nearby.

"If I just knew how the locket worked. Then I could find Pappy." Danny said.

"Give it time Poindexter, you'll figure it out and if you can't I'm sure one of us will when we get back to the school."

"Thanks, Dez."

"No problem. If you ever mention to Guy I was this nice to you, I'll deny every word and make you wish you were never born."

Danny laughed at this. "I'm going to let go of the locket now, so be ready."

"What do-"

Dez never got to finish her sentence because Danny had let go of the locket. The two of them found themselves hurtling back toward the cabin. Danny was prepared, but Dez was not.

Smack! Dez landed hard on the cabin floor. "Oh," She groaned. "Poindexter!"

Danny laughed and jumped back before Dez could pull herself off the ground. She charged at Danny but stopped just short of tackling him.

Freezing, she stared past Danny and at the glass wall. Just behind Danny, the wall was shattered into pieces and glass shards covered the floor.

Danny kept laughing, "Oh come on Dez, I'm not that fragile. I can take a hit."

Without saying anything Dez raised a hand and pointed at the wall.

Danny turned around and his jaw dropped. *How did that happen?*

Blood-curdling shrieks filled the air. The intensity of the shrieks increased with every passing second. It was the cry of Water Orcs.

Looking around the cabin Danny noticed Connor was nowhere to be seen. *Dang, it!* Had he tricked them, just like Fake Chase?

"Dez!" Danny yelled shakily. "What do we do?"

"Retreat!" Dez yelled back. "Follow me."

Dez scooped up one of the enchanted hammers that was laying on the closest bed. She had Danny right on her toes as they exited the front door of the cabin. Before Danny could ask her where they were going a Water Orc jumped out in front of them.

Dez swung the hammer, catching the Water Orc under the chin on an uppercut. *Crack*! The Water Orc went flying off the deck over the railing.

"Wow! That was incredible!"

Dez smiled. "Hey, you're still wearing the speed shoes! Find the trabea punctum. There are caves by the girl's cabins."

"What about you?"

"Don't worry about me. I can handle myself," Dez took another swing with the hammer as a Water Orc jumped out in front of her. "Just get to the trabea punctum. Connor is hopefully there."

"I can't leave you! Besides, he doesn't believe in the trabea punctum." Danny dodged another Water Orc.

"Go! You'll just slow me down," Dez said.

"What are you going to do?"

"Guy's duffle bag is still under his bed; I'm going to get us some real fire power. Go, Poindexter!" Dez commanded as she knocked out another Water Orc with the enchanted hammer.

Danny spun around in the direction of the girls' cabins only to come face-to-face with a Water Orc. He jumped back and then sprang forward, flattening the Water Orc as he sped to the mountains.

He slid to a stop just at the base of the mountain. Looking above, he searched for any sign of caves up top. How was he going to climb up there? He had never climbed anything before in his life.

Then he looked down to his feet. That's right, he had just used the speed shoes to make it across camp in less than a second. Surely, he could run up the mountain without any issues. Where was the cave?

Some debris from above rolled down the mountainside. Danny walked over to where it had fallen from. Directly above him, he could see the entrance of a cave. Stepping back, he was able to get a better view. Sure enough, it was a cave on the side of a mountain.

Dare he run up the mountain? Would he make it? What lay inside?

Danny wished he could think about it, but the shrieks from the other side of the camp were getting louder. This meant the Water Orcs were on the move and coming his way. He had no choice.

He had to gain momentum, to be certain he could make it up the mountain because if he failed… Well, Danny didn't want to think about that. He ran back to the mess hall and around it without slowing. Coming to the base of the mountain he did not decelerate but rather lunged at the base taking large strides.

Jack and the Beanstalk, Jack and the Beanstalk, he kept thinking over and over.

One step… Two steps… He was halfway to the cave… He was a step away. Danny changed his footing, as his first foot landed on the cave floor there was a loud, *smack!* Danny ran face-first into a rock full of wall. He had made it into the cave but failed to stop.

Man did his head hurt. As he lay on the floor of the cave, he noticed some shadowy figures approaching him. Danny was too dizzy to get up. What had he gotten himself into?

Chapter 10

The figures got closer to him. He was sure this was it.
"Hey! Over here!"
The figures stopped getting bigger.
Danny heard a *crack* and saw what looked like electricity flying through the air. He looked at where the electricity was coming from. There, behind the electricity were two shadowy figures. He tried to stand but was still weak from running into the rocky wall.
The two figures raced over to Danny.
Danny assumed one was Connor. "Am I glad to see you guys. How'd you escape?" Danny said groggily. His head was still throbbing. Slowly he rolled over and tried to push himself up. As he was doing this Connor grabbed him helping him stand.
"Hold him still," said a voice he did not recognize.
Things were still blurry, but he could tell someone stood in front of him as Connor stood next to him, propping him up.

"Danny, open your mouth… You need water." It was Connor's voice. "Just open your mouth up a little, so Lexi can give you some."

When Danny heard this, he immediately clenched his jaw shut. Now he questioned if it was really Connor beside him or a Water Orc imitating Connor.

"Got it, hurry." Connor had inched Danny's mouth open just by a bit.

Lexi grabbed her water pouch. She opened it and trickled some water into Danny's mouth.

Immediately, Danny's vision became better, his head stopped hurting, and he could stand.

"What was that?" He asked, realizing this must have been the real Connor and Lexi. If they were Water Orcs, he would surely have ended up frozen like everyone else.

"Water from the Fountain of Youth." Connor patted Danny on the back. "How are you feeling?"

"It heals?" Danny asked astounded.

"Yep, a few drops of this and it heals. One gulp and it makes you five years younger. Drink too much and you're right back to where you started in life. An infant." Lexi stated.

"Wow, that is so cool!"

Connor smiled, "I know, right? You should see-"

"Guys let's not get off track. There's a reason you called me." Lexi pointed her staff at three unchanged Water Orcs on the ground."

"Oh, right!" Connor replied.

"And it looks like you forgot to mention something." Lexi looked irritably at the back cave wall which was cracking open. In between the cracks blue light streamed through them.

Danny noticed the cracks were different sizes and when you looked at them altogether it was like a reverse puzzle. This must have been the trabea punctum. Fantasy world was breaking through.

"Hey, how was I supposed to know trabea punctums were real? They're supposed to be legends," Connor shrugged.

Lexi huffed, "Legends are real."

"Hey, don't act like you have ever come across a legend. They're no written records of them," Connor stated.

"Connor for being so smart you believe some foolish stuff. Just because there is no written record of them does not mean legends don't exist. We are standing right in front of one."

"Lexi, this is not the time for another lecture," Connor said exhaustively.

Lexi walked to the cave entrance, "Fine, let's start with the Water Orcs."

Danny looked out the cave entrance too. From up here one could see all of camp. The damage the Water Orcs had done to camp was a sorrowful sight. Water Orcs were not only on the beach, but in the woods, on top of cabins, and now they were starting to climb the mountain. *I shouldn't have left Dez.*

"Well, that's why I called you," Connor said. "I figured you could use your staff and just hit them all with some lightning. You know, stun them and they'll go back under the rock that they crawled out from."

"It's not that easy," Lexi turned to the back of the cave wall. "Since this is a trabea punctum that means the rest of the legend about them must be real. My lightning would only split the back of the cave wall creating a larger entrance in and out of Fantasy World. We would never get the trabea puntum closed.

Danny walked closer to the cave wall, examining it closely, "What do we need to close it?"

"According to legend, the best way to close one is a a pan flute," Lexi replied.

"Well, did you bring one?" Connor asked.

"No, someone forgot to mention the trabea punctum," Lexi shot back.

"Hey, how was I supposed to know they actually existed?" Connor mumbled.

"Well, do you happen to have a pan flute?" Lexi asked.

"There might be one on the submarine, but it may be full of Water Orcs." Connor replied.

Lexi let out an *argh*. "You and Chase are useless."

Danny was still looking out over the landscape when he saw her. Well, at least he thought he saw her. Her being Dez. "Hey! I know where we can get one or at least I think I do."

Lexi was astonished at this news, "You? You have a pan

flute?"

"Well, not on me, but I think Dez may have one."
Danny pointed at a little dot that was making its way
toward them. It was Dez zigzagging between Water Orcs,
every now and then stopping to crush one.

"That's great. If we can close this, then I can use my
staff to send the Water Orcs home."

"What about the campers? What will it do to them?"
Danny had to be sure the other campers and his friends
were safe.

"It won't do anything and once the Water Orcs get
further away the campers will start thawing out," Lexi
shared.

"That's great!" Danny exclaimed. "Let's get down there
and reach Dez."

Lexi jumped from the side of the mountain with her staff
in hand.

Danny took a deep breath. "Jack and The Beanstalk," he
said under his breath. With that, he took off running toward
Dez.

Connor, though, did not move. Instead, he yelled down
the mountain, "Looks like you guys have everything. I'll
just guard the trabea punctum and make sure it doesn't
open any wider," Truthfully, he was scared. He had already
been captured by the Water Orcs once.

Danny slid in next to Dez, who was crouched by a big
boulder. She was clutching the goblin bag and wearing the
lifting gloves he had seen earlier. "Where's the hammer?"

He asked.

Dez flexed her hand. "I upgraded. Hercules lifting gloves. These things really pack a punch. I'm as strong as a demigod," she said with a smirk. "Wait, I thought I told you to get to the caves and find the trabea punctum," She huffed.

"I did and now I need the goblin bag," Danny said reaching for the bag.

"No way am I giving this thing to you." Dez's eyes were now darting back and forth. She had found Lexi and was watching her bob and weave through the Water Orcs.

Lexi wielded her staff like it was a third arm. She spun twice around like a ballerina taking out Water Orcs from every angle. One by one the Water Orcs went soaring through the air and hit the ground.

"Wow, who is she?" Dez said with amazement.

"No time to explain. Do you have a pan flute in there?" Danny asked.

"Why a pan flute?" Dez questioned.

Danny was about to answer, but before he could Lexi yelled out, "Can you two hurry up, I can only keep this up for so long!"

Dez set the bag down. "Watch my back." She dived head-first into the goblin bag.

It was like Danny's head was on a swivel as he tried to watch everything. One minute ticked by, then another, then another. "Come on Dez, do you see one?"

Dez popped her head out of the bag, "Bingo!" She held

up a pan flute.

Danny grabbed the pan flute, "Got it!" He ran towards Lexi.

"Great! Now get it to Connor," Lexi commanded.

"I thought you were going to do it," Danny replied.

"Are you kidding me?" Lexi continued to knock over Water Orcs, "Connor's been playing the pan flute before he could ride a sea turtle. Give it to him. He's our best bet. Have him play Do-Re-Mi until the trabea punctum completely closes."

Lexi turned her attention back to the Water Orcs fully as Danny ran towards the caves. Halfway up the mountain, Danny started to slow, he did not want to smack into the back of the cave again. He turned his foot and stepped onto the cave floor. Although he had slowed, he was still coming in fast. Luckily, Connor was standing right there, and Danny ran into Connor pushing him back a few feet.

"Woah there Danny," Connor was able to stay on his feet.

"I've got it. The pan flute," Danny tossed the musical instrument to Connor.

Before the pan flute reached Connor, he was tackled to the ground by Fake Chase who was with New Guy and Imposter Ozzie. Right away Connor tried to get up but was shoved down by New Guy.

Danny's stomach turned at the sight of the three of them. *Shoot! And we're so close!* He ran and dove at the flute. With the flute in hand, Danny thought his best bet would be to get it to Dez or Lexi. As he got up Imposter Ozzie swung at the pan flute knocking it out of his hands.

New Guy picked up the pan flute and started playing it. The cracks in the rocks expanded as he played Do-Re-Mi backwards. As the cracks expanded Danny could see more of the fantasy world.

Outside the cave the bright sun was covered by dark clouds. Lightning and thunder filled the sky. Groans, shrieks, and squeaks echoed off the cave walls. Danny looked from the front of the cave to the back. Every creature he had ever read about in stories, and more were marching to the cave

Then he saw something, so unbelievable. *It can't be?* Then he saw it again, or rather the person again, *Pappy?*

Standing in front of the trabea punctum Danny was confused more than ever. Here Danny stood at the entrance of another world, and he swore he saw Pappy. In Danny's dream he had that night Pappy had told Danny he was in another world. That was it, his mind was just confused. *My mind is just playing tricks on me.*

Danny took a deep breath and turned away from the trabea punctum. He knew what he had to do; he had to take down the giant. Danny raced at New Guy, knocking him on the ground. With New Guy on the ground, Danny picked up the pan flute. He had never played one but had learned to play the recorder in elementary. *How hard can this be?*

Danny kept moving throughout the cave as he tried to play the pan flute. Moving made it hard for anyone to stop him from playing Do-Re-Mi but it also caused him to mess up a lot. After a few tries though, he could see it. The blue light from the back of the cave was fading.

Danny began to relax as he saw the **trabea punctum close.** He lost focus and stumbled over the cave floor. The pan flute flew out of his hands and hit the floor. He dove in hopes to regain the pan flute and seal the trabea punctum. Rather, his fingertips knocked the edge of it which only caused the pan flute to skid further away and into a gap in the cave wall.

Connor was now up and grappling with Fake Chase.

Danny rolled over only to see Imposter Ozzie's foot coming down on him. Continuing to roll, Imposter Ozzie's foot missed Danny by inches. Standing up Danny found New Guy running right for him. Before they collided though Dez came flying through the air and connected a hard right to New Guy's jaw. New Guy hit the ground hard though Dez did not let up, dropping the goblin bag she clutched in her other hand.

Danny ran to the wall where the pan flute was wedged under. He was about to lay himself flat when he was hit from behind, it was Imposter Ozzie. Danny turned ready to dodge another swing from him but did not have to. Lexi stuck out her staff and blocked Imposter Ozzie's next strike.

"Go, get the pan flute," Lexi commanded.

Danny laid down flat on his belly. It was too dark; he could not see how far back it had gone under the unmovable wall. "I can't see it!" Danny yelled.

"Here! Take a glove." Dez, still battling New Guy, took off one of Hercules' gloves and flung it in Danny's direction.

The glove floated a little way away from Danny. Luckily, he was wearing the speed shoes. He ran to catch the glove. He slipped the glove on and then ran back to the cave wall that the pan flute was stuck under.

He knelt down, made a fist, and pulled back his arm. *I hope this works. If not, I'm going to need a lot more Fountain of Youth Water.* With that, Danny let his hand fly as he hit the rock with all his might. The cave shook and the rock wall began to crumble. Along with it though, so did the rest of the cave.

Debris from the cave ceiling started falling. At first, it was like dust, but then the rocks started getting bigger. The ground really started to tremble. Then the whole mountain shook.

"Earthquake. Everyone out here." Lexi yelled.

Connor and Fake Chase sprinted for the front of the cave and slid down the hill. Neither looked back as they ran. Imposter Ozzie was slung over Lexi's shoulder as she had knocked him out. Dez took one last swing at New Guy which sent him flying to safety and out of the cave.

Dez turned to Danny, "Poindexter, let's go!"

"The pan flute though!" Danny shouted back as the magnitude of the earthquake grew.

"Don't worry about it. The trabea punctum is caving in

on itself. We don't need the pan flute. Nothing's going to come out of the trabea punctum, especially when the cave has crumbled."

"I know, but I can't let something this valuable be lost," Danny fired back.

"Poindexter, you've got to be kidding me. Those are a dime a dozen. Now put those speed shoes to good use and let's go!" Dez yelled as she picked up the goblin bag.

Realizing a pan flute was not worth his life or Dez's, he took to step towards her. As he ran past her, he grabbed her hand and went running down the mountain with her floating behind him from his speed.

The two of them made it to the front of the mess hall where everyone was already waiting for them. Lexi had tossed the unconscious Imposter Ozzie on the ground. Connor was twirling a fidget spinner in hand with Fake Chase and New Guy tied up next to him.

"How'd you do that?" Danny asked, referring to the electricity that bound Fake Chase and New Guy.

"Oh, you mean the electricity?" Connor smiled and continued to spin the fidget spinner. "Lexi's staff isn't the only thing that is electrifying."

"Yeah, they're the Atlantean version of handcuffs," Lexi added.

"Yeah, great for questioning too. Like where's my brother, you little weasels?" Connor asked.

"Yeah, where are all the others?" Dez shot daggers at the Water Orcs.

Just then there was a low hum.

The hairs on Danny's neck stood up. *That's right, we're still surrounded by Water Orcs.*

Fake Chase and New Guy laughed.

"You better let us go or you four are next and once you go. There will be no one to save you." Fake Chase stated.

"Oh, I wouldn't worry about us." Lexi said.

"Yeah, we've had worse odds." Dez smirked.

Danny looked around. Not only were they surrounded by Water Orcs on the ground, but in the trees, and more came from the water. He gulped. They were doomed.

Chapter 11

Lexi pulled her staff from her sling ready to fight. "You three get inside."

"Nah ah, you're not having all the fun," Dez said slyly. "Poindexter, give me the other glove."

Lexi did not have to tell Danny twice to get inside. He pulled Hercules' glove off his hand and gave it to Dez. "Have fun." He said, heading into the mess hall.

"You two," referring to Fake Chase and New Guy. "Let's go," Connor ordered.

"Suit yourself, ladies." New Guy remarked before entering the mess hall.

Connor sat New Guy and Fake Chase over in a corner where they could not see the outside. Danny on the other hand stared out the windows where he could see everything.

Dez secured Hercules' gloves by tugging at them.

Lexi wielded her staff around her. "I go high, you stay low."

"Deal" Dez replied as she charged forward.

Lexi jumped into the air and landed on a tree branch. She bounded from tree branch to tree branch striking Water Orcs all along the way while Dez stayed on the ground. On the ground, Dez was pummeling Water Orcs left and right.

Inside, Danny stood there with his mouth hanging open, "Do you see this Connor?"

Connor looked up for a second. "Yeah, this is nothing new to me. Told you we'd only need Lexi." Turning his attention back to Fake Chase and New Guy, Connor asked, "So do you want to tell me where our friends are, or are we just going to have to send you all home first?"

"Ha, nice try, but you won't get a word out of us," Fake Chase replied.

Connor laughed, "You do remind me of my brother with *that* attitude. Though, that is where the similarities between you and him end. He would never talk but a Water Orc. Well, there are ways of making you talk… You're all water in your original form. We both know water and electricity don't exactly play well. Do they?"

Connor started spinning the fidget faster and as he did the electric rope tying Fake Chase and New Guy up began to increase in intensity. They both groaned in pain and their bodies glitched in and out, alternating from host form to Water Orc form.

Connor slowed the fidget spinner. "Where are they?"

"Never!" New Guy growled.

Connor spun the fidget spinner faster. The electricity

flared up again and the Water Orcs' groans switched to shrieks.

"One last time," Connor said as the fidget spinner slowed.

The Water Orcs were panting hard and had turned back to their original form for good.

"They're in your submarine." One of the Water Orcs said.

"Good luck getting on and getting off in one piece." The other said.

"See now, was that so hard?" Connor grabbed the electric rope by the hand and dragged the Water Orcs to the mess hall entrance. "Danny, start pulling the frozen campers out of the cooler and setting them in front of the ovens."

"Should I turn the ovens on?" Danny asked.

"Oh, you'll know when. Just keep an eye on Lexi and Dez. I'm heading to the submarine to free my brother and your friends."

"What about those two?" Danny pointed to the two tied up Water Orcs.

"Oh, they'll just sit outside with all the others." Connor smirked as he pulled the Water Orcs through the doors.

"Wait, wait, we're sorry. We've got more to tell!"

"Yeah, we can tell you who sent us."

"Blah, blah, blah, I don't care." Danny could hear Connor say as the mess hall door shut behind them.

Danny darted to the windows again and looked out

front. Dez was walking up to the two Water Orcs Connor had just brought out. Danny scanned for Connor but could not find him. Danny ran through the kitchen swinging door, looking out the windows now that faced the beach. Connor was running towards the water. He got to the shoreline and jumped right in.

Connor dove under the water and all Danny could see were wake waves, like from a speed boat leading out to the center of the lake. The waves stopped and Connor dove down to his submarine. Since Danny could not see anymore, nor help Connor, he decided to start taking the campers out of the cooler.

He opened the cooler door, and there staring back at him were campers, frozen like human popsicles. Danny found the dolly. One by one he put campers on the dolly and raced them out to the main kitchen, setting them gently in front of the stove.

As he did this, he counted each trip he took. *38...42...46... 47.* He was only halfway through and still was not tired, in fact, he was getting faster as he went. It must have been the shoes, he figured. 96...108...116. There were 116 campers and counselors packed into the walk-in cooler along with Mr. and Mrs. Dodd and Mr. Kirby. *Wow!*

Danny sped out of the kitchen and back to the front of the mess hall. Looking out the front windows he saw what Connor was talking about. Connor's voice replayed in Danny's head, *You'll know when.*

Lightning shot out of Lexi's staff in every direction. All the Water Orcs in the trees fell from the branch they were perched on. Dez swung her arms back and clapped her hands together with as much force as she could. The Water Orcs on the ground fell over like bowling pins.

All the Water Orcs were laying on the ground and all had shifted back to their original form. Dez gave one last clap, and a lot of the Water Orcs were pushed into the lake. Lexi's staff lit up once again striking any Water Orcs left on the beach. The electricity jolted the Water Orcs awake. Without hesitation, the remaining Water Orcs ran to the lake and dove into the water.

Danny stood there forgetting he had a job to do. He watched as waves crashed against the shoreline and Water Orcs headed out of the lake. Finally, he snapped out of it. *The ovens.* He raced back into the kitchen and turned the ovens on. Once they were all on, he opened the oven doors and heat poured out.

Shoot! What do we tell everyone? They're going to wonder why they're all soaking wet. And the avalanche outside.

Danny ran out to Lexi and Dez. "Guys, what do we tell everyone?"

Dez ran to the goblin bag. "Are they awake, yet?"

"I don't think so," Danny replied.

"Give me a second." Dez ruffled around inside the goblin bag. She popped her head out of the goblin bag and triumphantly held up a little bottle of sand. "Yes, got it!"

"What is it?" Danny wondered.

"Sand from the Sandman!" Dez exclaimed proudly.

Danny stared at her blankly.

"You know, the Sandman from dreamland?"

"Huh?" Danny had no clue what Dez was talking about.

"You've got to be kidding me, Poindexter!" Dez was shocked.

"Sorry." He shook his head.

"Here." Dez handed Danny the bottle of sand. "Just go in there and sprinkle some sand on everyone before they thaw and wake up. As they wake, they will think this is all a dream and just head back to their cabins."

"Clever," Danny smirked.

"It won't be unless you get a move on. Now go! Run!" Dez shooed Danny away.

With the bottle of sand in hand, Danny ran off. He weaved through the crowd of human popsicles sprinkling sand on every one of them. Standing back, he admired his handy work. Campers and counselors started coming awake and as each one did, they either yawned or stretched. They looked around in a daze and then just walked off to find their bed.

Danny smiled. *Finally*, he thought.

"What is going on?" A voice bellowed.

Danny turned his head left and then right. He did not see who asked that, though by the time he looked forward he was staring at someone's chest. It was Mr. Dodd.

"What is going on here boy?" Mr. Dodd asked. "I want

answers now!"

Danny could not find the words to explain, stepping back he tried to think.

"Mr. Dodd!" Dez yelled from across the kitchen.

Mr. Dodd spun around.

Dez walked up to them, without an ounce of worry she said, "It's a dream, Mr. Dodd. That's all. When you wake up in a while, you'll find this is just all a dream."

"This is all a dream." Mr. Dodd repeated and walked off.

Once again, Danny was stunned at what Dez could do. "How'd you do that?"

"Honestly Poindexter." She shook her head. "You have a lot to learn. Come on, let's go find Guy and Ozzie."

"Race you!" Danny said.

Before Dez could say anything, Danny was out of the mess hall and already standing by the lake.

Dez sprinted through one of the mess hall doors and out to the beach, "That was not fair."

"Who said anything about fair?" Danny smirked.

"Look, they're coming," Lexi pointed at the lake.

Sure enough, two wake waves were coming in from the center of the lake and right up to the shoreline. Connor and Chase came strolling out of the water. One supporting Guy and the other supporting Ozzie. Guy and Ozzie collapsed once they got on the beach.

Danny, Dez, and Lexi walked up to them.

"What happened?" Chase asked.

"Exactly what you said," Danny stated.

"Danny, that's Chase. I'm over here." Connor waved his hands around.

"Oh… You two *are* identical."

"Dude, I still don't understand what happened," Chase said.

"We happened; Lexi and I." Dez let the group know.

"Tubular…And you might be?" Chase flashed a smile.

Yep, dude… tubular… This was the real Chase, Danny thought.

"I'm Dez. You must be Chase, right?"

"The one and only." His smile still beaming, Chase shook Dez's hand.

"Ha, I wouldn't say that." Connor laughed. "For a while, there were four of us. Two of me and two of you."

"Yeah, but none of them look this good." Chase flipped his blonde surfer hair back and struck a pose like he was a lifeguard from that old 90's TV show Danny's mom always rewatched.

Connor shoved his brother playfully. "Be quiet man," he said with a grin.

Chase shoved his brother back even harder, "No you stop it, man." He laughed.

"Dude, I missed you," Connor said.

"Bro, you're telling me. That Connor was a real drag. No fun at all," Chase replied.

Looking up at the group, Guy asked between heavy breaths, "What does cleanup look like?"

"Poindexter here demolished the mountain with one of Hercules gloves here… Lexi and I demolished the Water Orcs," Dez smirked at sharing this news.

"Anyone hurt?" Guy asked, still trying to catch his breath.

"Negative. I had Poindexter here use the Sandman's sand to make everyone think it's a dream."

"Really? Still going with Poindexter," Danny asked. Dez nodded. "Yes, sir."

Guy turned to Ozzie. "Ozzie, how are you holding up?"

"I think I'm going to hurl." Ozzie groaned as he leaned over clutching his stomach.

"Oh, sorry about that Oz Man," Chase crouched down to Ozzie's level. "It's from Connor and me swimming so fast. Humans can't put up with the change in pressure like Atlanteans. If you eat it should get better."

"Food does not sound good," Ozzie replied.

"Lexi, do you still have any of your water?" Connor asked.

"Yeah." Lexi replied.

"Pour some in my hand." Connor held out his hand.

Lexi put a tablespoon of water in Connor's hand. Connor knelt next to Ozzie. "Here, drink this."

"No," Ozzie groaned.

"Ozzie, trust me. It'll make you feel better," Connor pushed his hand forward.

Ozzie stretched his neck out and took a sip of water from Connor's hand. Instantly, Ozzie sprang up. "Wow!

That stuff is incredible. Can I have some more?"

Lexi laughed, "Not a chance."

Chapter 12

"Can you pass me the potatoes?"

"Could I get some chicken over here?"

"Make sure you save room for dessert.

The mess hall was empty except for Danny and his friends. Everyone else was still sleeping from the sand Danny had hit them all with but he and his friends were starving. Luckily the walk-in cooler was stocked full of food and the kitchen was ready to be used. Everyone in the group pitched in to cook something and now they were all sitting around a table enjoying their meal.

"So, you're telling me you've faced Water Orcs before?" Chase asked.

"Yep!" Dez said with a smile.

"You've got to be kidding me." Chase shouted back to Connor who was walking up to the table. "Dez here says, this isn't their first encounter with Water Orcs."

"And goblins, elves, vampires, werewolves, and the list goes on." Dez touted.

"Okay Dez, that's enough," Guy said. Turning to Lexi he asked, "So did you find out why the Water Orcs were here? Or who sent them?"

Lexi held up a finger to Guy signaling one second. She finished chewing, "Two words, trabea punctum."

Guy dropped his fork upon hearing the words. "What about them?"

"They're real." Lexi replied.

"Yeah, we saw one," Dez said through a mouth full of mashed potatoes.

"You saw one, here?" Guy asked stunned. "But I thought legends weren't real."

"That's what I said," Connor shouted from across the table. "Man, was I wrong."

Danny, Dez, and Lexi all nodded their heads yes, to indicate they were real.

"How is one here?" Guy asked.

"Not too sure how it got here. My guess is it's always been here. I do believe it's the first one to ever be found and opened." Lexi replied. "Don't worry, though, Danny here closed it."

"Yeah, you should have seen it. Poindexter played the pan flute like a champ. Best rendition of **Do-Re-Mi**, yet." Dez shared.

Danny blushed at this. It was nice to hear Dez compliment him, he did not even mind she was calling him Poindexter.

"Jack and the Beanstalk, right Danny?" Guy yelled

across the table with a smile. Everyone looked at Guy in bewilderment. "Don't worry, Danny knows."

Danny nodded in Guy's direction; he knew exactly what Guy meant. He meant that Danny, like Jack, had believed in himself to take down the giant. Just like Jack did in the story.

"What else did Ozzie and I miss?" Guy asked.

"Really that was it. Just closing the trabea punctum." Dez said.

"Do we know if more trabea punctums are out there?" Guy questioned before biting into a piece of chicken.

"Well, we do have a lead on some Water Orcs meeting up with some of their cousins, the Mountain Orcs, near the Alps." Lexi shared.

Danny's ears perked up at this news. "The Alps?"

"Yeah. I wouldn't worry about it too much, man. Orcs are always visiting one another," Chase shared.

"Yeah, not this many though?" Lexi asked. "My dad says he hasn't seen this many Water Orcs in the Alps in a millennium."

"How many are we talking about?" Danny shakily asked.

"A hundred at least, and they are going from one region to another." Lexi said. "We have our eye on them though. That's actually where my dad is right now."

"You mean King Atlas?" Dez shrieked excitedly.

"Yes, King Atlas. He is there on a formality though more for diplomatic relations. If we hear anything we will be sure to contact your advisor, Allen Dailey."

Danny gulped again. "Wait, you know Allen Dailey?"

Dez laughed, "Of course they do, everyone knows your grandpa."

"Dude, Allen Dailey is your grandpa?" Chase bellowed.

"Yep," Danny said sheepishly.

"Dude, your-"

Lexi kicked Chase under the table before he could finish his sentence.

"Ow! Why'd you do that?"

If Danny had looked up from his plate, he would have seen Lexi mouthing the word *quiet*, to Chase. Danny, however, was too embarrassed to look in their direction. *Of course, they know Pappy, why not? He's a legend.*

"So, Danny, how is your grandpa?" Lexi asked in hopes to divert Danny's attention from what Chase was about to say.

"He's good." Danny lied. "He's off on a mission." *No, he's not*, Danny thought. He's *disappeared into another world for all I know, and that world could be Fantasy World… And I might have just closed his only way home.* Danny shook his head. *No, my mind was playing tricks on me earlier and that was a dream last night, just a dream… It felt so real though.*

"Well, when you see him can you tell him Lexi, Connor, and Chase say *hi.*"

"Yeah, we sure do miss seeing him." Chase replied.

Lexi kicked Chase under the table again. Once again,

Danny was too deep in thought to notice.

Yeah, if I ever see him. "Will do!" Danny put on a fake smile.

"Well, this has been great, but we've got to get going," Lexi got up from the table and headed to the kitchen to put her empty tray away.

Guy got up and did the same, "So, I'll send you a full report once my team debriefs and gets back to the school."

"Sounds good. I'll make sure we do the same," Lexi tossed her tray into an empty sink. "Connor, Chase, let's get a move on. I want to make it home before my mom realizes where I took the cruiser."

Connor and Chase came racing through the door with the rest of the group in tow. All of them tossed their trays in a sink and then headed out the back of the mess hall.

Walking towards the water they could see something bubbling to the surface. The top of the water broke as Chase and Connor's submarine appeared. The submarine looked nothing like a submarine that humans were used to seeing, rather this one was shaped like a flying saucer; sleek and shiny.

The submarine rose until it was in the air. Once it was a few feet above the ground a bay door opened.

"Woah, this is so cool!" Ozzie said. "Can I go in?"

Chase looked as though he was going to say yes, that was until he looked at Lexi. Her face clearly said no. "Another time Oz Man, I promise."

"Yeah, we really have to get going." Lexi said.

"We always have time for a goodbye though. Hugs anyone?" Chase asked.

"I'll take one." Dez ran at Chase with so much speed she almost tackled him.

"Sure, why not?" Guy said as he gave Connor a half hug.

Even Danny and Ozzie got in on the goodbyes. The two of them did not seem as much into it as the rest. Danny because his mind was preoccupied with Pappy. Ozzie because he was not the biggest on hugs.

"Call me," Chase shouted to Dez as he walked to the bay door and on to the submarine.

"Will do!" Dez said, holding up a seashell that he had given her.

"Bye guys!" Guy waved. "Thanks for the help."

Danny waved goodbye but did not say anything. He was still trying to make sense of the thought of Water Orcs searching the Alps. Pappy was just there last summer gathering the enchanted books that were now in Adam's possession. Danny knew the Water Orcs scaling the Alps was not a coincidence and was worried Pappy was in more trouble than he knew.

Danny had to get news to Pappy, he had to warn him. Something bigger was coming. For now, though, he wanted to take this time and enjoy it with his new friends. He wanted to celebrate his victory.

"What are you thinking, Danny?" Guy asked with a smile.

"Not sure… I guess what's next?" Danny smiled back.

"Next, we write the story."

<u>About the Author</u>
Brian Everest lives in the Midwest with his wife Tillie and two cats: Toph & Katara. He enjoys time with family, friends, writing, and traveling.

<u>Other books by Brian Everest</u>

Coming soon:

<u>Book 3:</u>
Scan the School:
The Fourth Estate